Entangled
with Faeries

Book 3

Lynn Donovan

Copyright

This book is a work of fiction. The names, characters, places, and incidents are all products of the author's imagination and are not to be construed as real. Any resemblances to persons, organizations, events, or locales are entirely coincidental.

The book contains material protected under International and Federal Copyright Laws and Treaties. All rights are reserved with the exceptions of quotes used in reviews. No part of this book may be reproduced or transmitted in any form or by any means, electronic or mechanical, including photocopying, recording, or by any information storage system without express written permission from the author.

Dedication

To Abbie Jane

Appreciation

Thank you to everybody in my life who has contributed in one way or another to the writing of this book. My husband, my children, my children-in-law, and my grandchildren. You all are my unconditional fans. My BETA readers, writers' group, and grammar guru who make me look gooder than I am. [Bad grammar intended.] My fellow author friends who chat with me daily to exchange ideas, encourage, maintain sanity, and keep me from being a total recluse/hermit.

Mostly, I thank God for the talent he has given me. I hope to hear you say, "Well done, my good and faithful servant," when I cross the Jordan and run into your arms—Many, many years from now. God bless you all!

Chapter One

"Hey!" Abbie Crossan tucked a strand of bright pink hair behind her ear and rapped her knuckle on the glass wall of the Absolutely Sterile Environment laboratory. "You ready for lunch, Sis?"

Karole Crossan looked up from a microscope. Red-ringed impressions still lingered around her eyes. "Oh! Hey."

She slipped her bronze wire-framed glasses on and glanced at the only decoration on the stark white wall, an extra-large black and white clock. "Is it lunch time already?"

Abbie snickered at the fading rosy raccoon mask as her sister prepared to leave the ASE lab. Karole might be a medical doctor who graduated with honors, but she was still her geeky older sister. Karole slid out of her green medical lab coat and tossed it in a container marked "WFD."

Apparently it was a joke for the medical lab only. Abbie had worked with this Variable Entanglement

Investigation at Loville facility for three years and her sister had just come on board two weeks ago, yet Karole refused to explain it to Abbie. The VEIL facility had so many acronyms they had formed an acronym department. But Abbie couldn't find WFD listed anywhere.

Karole stepped into the small decontamination chamber the size of a phone booth. In fact, Abbie had helped the medical team a year ago to paint it to look like the TARDIS. That had been when she was dating one of the doctors, but it felt like a life time or two before this one.

The door to the chamber sealed shut and a white fog engulfed Karole, starting at her feet, and dissipated through the ceiling air return system. Abbie always wished her sister would emerge from the mist in a faerie costume, like Tinker Bell, but it never happened.

Karole stepped into the outer laboratory to give Abbie a hug. Abbie leaned back with her nose wrinkled. "That leaves such a weird smell on you. I'm glad I don't have to do that every time I leave my office."

Karole shrugged. "You get used to it, I guess. Besides, why would dirt diggers need an ASE?"

"I'm a geologist, not a dirt digger!" Abbie glared at her. "And you'd be surprised what we can get exposed to digging in ancient layers of sediment, in fact, my stratigraphical analysis of this mountain—"

Karole waved the old argument off. "I'm sorry, I'm

just tired. Please don't explain your studies on the strata in this mountain to me again. Even now that I work here, I still don't… care."

Abbie stared at her sister, the words still hanging in her mouth. "Yeah, I'm not in a good mood either." Abbie pondered the sterilizing booth. "I wonder? If I didn't come by to get you, would you eat?"

"Probably not. Besides, I'm still feeling out a routine. But think of all the weight I'd lose not going by your stomach's insistent clock."

They laughed.

"Yeah, that's called starvation, Karole, not weight loss."

"Well, good thing I have you to keep me nourished." She glanced around the office and patted her ID badge hanging from a lanyard around her neck. "Okay, I'm ready."

Abbie wrapped her arm around her sister's shoulder and led the way. "When are you going to divulge the secret code for the WFD?"

Karole's eyes twinkled. "It's above your pay grade, dear sister."

Abbie shook her head. Together they exited the Medical building, walking toward the facility's cafeteria.

Karole ran a cursory eye down Abbie's length. Genuine interest washed over her face. "So, why are you in a bad mood?"

"Oh…" Abbie sighed heavily. "… I have a concern—maybe it's nothing." Abbie plucked an aspen leaf. Its gradient autumn transformation transposed from yellow to rust. Twisting it as they walked, she made it into a rose.

A groundskeeper smiled up at them from a dormant flowerbed she was attending. Karole scanned the indigenous garden between the buildings. "Mmm. It's so pretty here."

"Yes it is. Morning, Ling." Abbie greeted the groundskeeper with a smile and a nod.

Karole turned back to Abbie. "I'm sure you'll work it out."

"Yeah. I'm trying." Abbie tucked a strand of pink hair behind her ear along with the fiery flower.

"Can you feel the excitement in the air?" Karole looked around, as if she could actually see something sparkle in the atmosphere.

Abbie sighed again. "Yeah. I think the physicists in QuCAD are getting close to a giga-breakthrough." She shook her head. "I just hope everything goes okay."

"You scientists and your acronyms. What's QuCAD again?"

"Quantum Chemistry Applications Department." Abbie chuckled. "Yeah, acronyms help keep our operations as obscure as possible."

Karole laughed. "That's the truth. Like our WFD container." Karole chortled. "I'll get the hang of it eventually, er, I mean, ASAP?" She walked sideways to make eye contact with Abbie. "Why wouldn't it?"

Abbie met her sister's gaze, confused. "Why wouldn't what?"

"Why wouldn't everything go okay?"

"Oh!" Abbie threw her head back. "Because! I don't know what WFD stands for and it may ruin everything as we know it!"

Karole shook her head as she continued walking at Abbie's side. "Stop that! From what I was told at orientation, the Quantum Entanglement Physics Lab is super safe, contained against the mountain, and Patrick said all of the component tests have been successful."

Abbie dropped her gaze to the ground. "I know… It's just— never mind."

"Patrick also said today's the day they're firing up the whole *shebang*." Karole smiled as they entered the dining hall.

"Interesting use of words. Is that what our little brother calls the Quantum Entanglement Super Toroid, the whole shebang?"

Karole opened her mouth wide as if with surprise. "Ha! I know that one! What you geeks call the 'QEST'."

Abbie glanced around the cafeteria. "That or just QuEST, like everybody else." Lowering her voice to a whisper, she grabbed her sister's arm. "Look. There *he* is!"

"Who?" Karole lifted a tray and placed it on the skid, then followed Abbie's line of sight. "How long are you going to admire that guy from afar? Go over there and introduce yourself!"

Abbie placed half a turkey-on-rye sandwich wrapped in a see-through cream-colored cloth on her tray along with a small Cobb salad and a little container of balsamic dressing.

Karole stared at the sandwich with disgust. "What is your sandwich wrapped in?"

Abbie glanced down at her selection. "It's Bee's Wrap, organic cotton muslin infused with beeswax, jojoba oil, and tree resin…" She leaned down to sniff the wrap. "… and lilac I believe. It's an environmentally safe alternative to plastic wrap."

Karole halted in moving down the food selection line and turned to Abbie with frustration gleaming in her eyes. "You guys implemented it? Didn't you?"

Abbie frowned. "I didn't. But yes, my department did."

"I suppose you environmental geeks can come up with all kinds of weird stuff to appease our overzealous environmentally conscious benefactors?"

Abbie smiled. "Job security. And no, I'm not going to just walk over there and introduce myself to that gorgeous man. What if he's married?"

Karole sighed and continued down the food selection line. "Well, if he is, then shame on him for not wearing a wedding ring."

"Some scientists don't— in fact lots of scientists don't wear jewelry! You know that. How many electrical burns have you treated in the ER over the years from electric arcs? Hum?" She bulged her eyes at her sister. "Or amputated what was left of a finger after a ring caught on a ladder spur and stripped the skin right off—"

"Okay. I get it." Karole cringed. "But still, he doesn't have that look."

"What look? Do men have a certain 'look' when they're married." Abbie stole a glance toward him.

"Yes. They do. And they put off a certain vibe."

"Certain vibe? Is that your medical opinion, Dr. Crossan?"

"Yes, it certainly is. Use that organ in your gut that only women have. Women's intuition is real, sister. What does that organ tell you about your Dr. Perfect?"

Abbie sighed dreamily. "That he's gorgeous…"

"Besides that?"

"He works in the QuCAD, that's Quantum Chemistry Applications Department to you who seem to be out of the lingo loop, and he's a PhD, and he has Extra Sensitive Information, Top Secret Clearance like you and me."

"Well, duh. I knew he worked in the QuCAD from his

red lab coat and that he's a PhD from his striped badge." Karole pressed her red ESI Top Secret Clearance badge to the point-of-sale scanner.

A pleasant mechanical voice responded when the transaction was accepted. "Thank you Doctor Karoley Crossan."

Karole rolled her eyes. "Remind me to talk to Patrick about changing the spelling of my name in the dietary POS system. I hate being called Karoley."

She looked at her badge. "Maybe you should talk to HR about implementing a bright red Ghostbuster's circle-and-slash on the badges to indicate MARRIED." Karole jerked as if she'd suddenly remembered something important. "Oh. I'm sorry go ahead, tell me what else you know about your dream man."

Abbie smiled. "I know that Dr. Perfect remembers to eat lunch."

"Okay… he doesn't have you to pester him into taking a lunch break, what else?"

"Not yet." Abbie smiled teasingly, then pursed her lips. "I don't know…" Abbie sat her tray down and eased into the chair, her eyes remained on the chemist."

"Will you just eat!" Karole unwrapped her sandwich.

"Okay." Abbie leaned her chin on her palm, still staring across the room. She absently pierced her salad with an organic disposable fork and stuffed the lettuce in her mouth.

"Didn't your dad teach you not to put your elbow on the table?" Karole pushed her sister's elbow and caused her head to lurch.

"My dad is your dad and you know it was Grandma who taught us table manners. Besides, after you moved out, Dad always let me eat on the couch."

"That's because you were the number two child who was allowed to juggle knives while jumping off the roof onto a trampoline without a side net or helmet. I was the guinea-pig-first-born who would have been swaddled in bubble-wrap if it had been legal." They laughed. "So you gonna go over and introduce yourself?"

"I might—" Abbie flushed with embarrassment. "Not."

"Oh for heaven's sake!" Karole leapt to her feet and marched across the cafeteria. "Excuse me."

Abbie rushed up behind her, pawing at her shoulder but missing.

"Hi." Karole stuck out her hand. "I'm Dr. Karole Crossan, from Medical. I don't believe we've met. You are…"

He looked up startled, wiped his mouth, and then stood. His smile exposed gleaming white teeth behind perfectly formed lips.

"I'm Dr. Joseph Assad." A hispanic accent rolled off

his tongue like a cat's purr. Abbie's legs turned to rubber. She flattened against her sister's backside, shoving her forward. Karole shoved back.

He leaned his head to look around Karole.

She grabbed Abbie's coat sleeve and pulled her around to face him.

"Hi." Abbie waved her hand like a windshield wiper set on high, then cleared her throat, and stood stiff as if drawing herself to attention. "Um, I'm Dr. Abbie Crossan. She's my sister. I-uh, I'm in QuESO, um, Quantum Environmental Studies and Operations… I'm uh, a uh ge- geologist. I-yuh…I like your lab coat."

He pursed his lips but smiled, as he turned his head slightly, keeping his amused gaze on Abbie. "Thanks. The facility provides them. I like your color selection for your hair. *Rosa* is… becoming on you."

Abbie touched her hair, squeezing her eyes closed, then opening them. "I, uh, I like pink…" She pulled her pale-yellow Environmental lab coat closed over the pink Tinker Bell t-shirt she had chosen that morning. Would he think she had a childish fetish? If only he knew how crazy she really was about the famous Disney character. Her Tinker Bell collection was more than a hobby, it was a solid quest in life. Pink was the color that made her feel happy.

As a geologist, she worked with dull, bland-tans, as she referred to her co-scientists' personalities. Bright pink balanced her soul and kept her from turning into one of them. Not that she didn't respect her fellow environmental workers, she just needed the effects of pink in her world.

Karole shoved her aside. "Well, we'll be going. Just wanted to introduce ourselves." She paused. "Say, we are getting together after work with some co-workers—"

"We are?" Abbie jerked her eyes toward her sister.

"Yes— for a drink, why don't you and your wife join us?"

His eyes widened, a slight blush filled his naturally sun-kissed cheeks. "Oh, I'm not married."

Abbie stepped in front of her sister. "Really? That's great… I mean… me neither."

Karole pushed her aside again. "Well, come join us. It's simply an opportunity to meet others who work here. This facility is like a lost city. There are so many of us, and most are new to the area." She chuckled. "We are all so focused on this Quantum Entanglement race we stay cooped up in our labs and don't get out to meet people. You should join us. It's a place on-site called *The Oasis*. It's at the East Gate."

"Oh. I don't know…"

"Pleeease!" Abbie lunged around her sister. "I mean please say you'll come. It's not good to work, work, work. Right, Dr. Crossan?"

Karole looked at her sister with incredulous eyes.

"Look, being a VEIL scientist is a focused and solitary life. I understand, but it's not healthy. You should get out and be around people."

He seemed to consider the validity of her advice.

"Listen, all work and no play— dull boy… you know? Doctor's orders." She took out a small note pad and wrote on it. "Here. This is a prescription for leisure time at The Oasis and no talking shop for at least Q2."

"Q-2? Oh, two hours?" He smiled.

"Yes. I encourage you to fill this tonight after work, say… seven o'clock?"

He took the paper and looked at what she wrote. A half smile raised one side of his mouth.

"Well… maybe." He lifted his eyes to Abbie. "You'll be there?"

"Me? Yeah. Of course. If you're there, I'll be there." Her hands balled into fists at her side. "I mean—"

Karole butted in, "Excuse my sister. She's not this awkward once you get to know her." She took Abbie's shoulder and pushed her as they clumsily walked away. Calling back to him over her shoulder, Karole said, "See you there tonight."

Abbie tripped over her own feet with her sister's insistent shoving, trying to see if he answered her final invitation. He smiled, watching them stagger away, and nodded.

"Yes!" Abbie pumped her hand at her side. "He said yes!"

They sat back down to their abandoned table with their abandoned food.

Abbie leaned toward her sister. "You think he meant it, or was he just being nice."

Karole sighed. "Man, you've got it bad."

"What?" Abbie stuffed a fork full of salad in her mouth and mumbled around the food. "I do not!"

"Are you kidding me? You were falling all over yourself!" She laughed. "Look, I don't know if he'll show up at The Oasis or not, but I can tell you this—"

Abbie leaned into her sister. "What?"

"If he does, then you'll know."

"Know what?"

"He's into you, too."

She flopped back against the chair. "Why would that tell me he's into me?"

"Because, little sister, if he comes to The Oasis, he's definitely in to you." She wrinkled her mouth, the way she always did when frustrated. "You acted like an idiot over there."

"Oh God. Was I that bad?" Abbie peeked over at Dr. Assad. He had finished his meal and stood with his tray.

Abbie sighed. "I blew it, didn't I?"

He walked to the dish return window and placed his

tray on the stainless steel counter. A young girl, sporting a hair net and gold Dietary Department coat, pulled the tray toward her and separated trash and food from dish, and stacked the plate in a washer rack. He said something to her. She looked up and smiled.

Abbie smiled too. She liked the idea that he was nice to the people who served in dietary. He turned. Abbie darted her eyes to the floor as he walked directly toward her and Karole's table. His smile widened and he tapped their table with the tip of his fingers as he walked past. He had a nice clean manicure. "Drs. Crossan. See you later."

Abbie stared with her mouth hanging open as he left the cafeteria. She patted her sister's arm with a fluttering hand. "He said, 'see us later!'"

Karole put her chin in her hand, elbow on the table. "That he did. At the very least, maybe he'll call you."

Abbie stiffened. Her brow furrowed. "Why do you say that?"

"That prescription I wrote him…"

Terror filled Abbie's heart. What had her sister done? She managed to utter, "Yeah?"

"I gave him *your* phone number."

Chapter Two

Abbie tapped the enter key with her little finger. The program ran the probabilities equations again. Every department head meeting she'd attended had left her frustrated and more worried. While the other scientists didn't ignore her reports, they certainly hadn't acted on them either. Her calculations to date haunted her logic. The mountain's strata analysis had definitely changed since the quantum experiments began. That couldn't be ignored.

While she waited for the compilations, she put her favorite K-cup pod in the Keurig and placed a coffee mug on the drip tray. Hazelnut-cinnamon soon filled the air. She sighed with pleasure at the aroma. At least something was coming out right today.

The program chimed, indicating 'End Program.' She quickly sipped a gulp of her coffee and rushed to see the output. Falling into her chair, she furrowed her brow. "This is not good."

She stepped up to her electronic white board and scratched out more equations based on this new data. The purple dry-erase marker squeaked under her hurried hand. She stood back and looked it over. "I've gotta go talk to Physics."

Pressing the share icon on the frame of the smart board, she transferred the equation to her secured tablet, tucked it under her arm, and left the QuESO building.

Every time she walked past the brass placard identifying her building she mused about her sister chastising her for the acronym. "Queso? Seriously? You named your department after cheese dip?"

"Look, it's the way of a top secret facility, such as VEIL, to use acronyms, why not have some fun with it? We've got to humanize this project! I can't think of a better way than to name my department Quantum Environmental Studies and Operations. It fits and it's funny at the same time. Besides those eggheads at HQ won't make the connection."

Abbie chuckled at the memory. She stepped into the indigenous garden. Ling, the environmental engineer, worked in an area of sculptured beds, under the aspen trees. Abbie walked along the pink crushed granite path toward the QuCAD. The Quantum Chemistry Application Department appeared to be a small building, but in truth it was built against this section of the Rocky Mountains, called Mount Herman.

It had been her first assignment when she came

onboard with the quantum facility planning team. Back then, she had officed in Loville's downtown area, between an ice cream shop and a new-age tea shop. Just a half dozen scientists and a few admin people.

Their purpose intentionally obscured by not updating the old tole-paint sign that read, "Janice's Jewelry & Junk." The quaint little town flourished with several antique shops and mom-and-pop restaurants along Main Street. Janice had moved to a bigger town for better retail opportunities. Little did ol' Janice know that big changes were soon to come to her small commerce.

It had been deemed a big secret that the private corporation, funded by private investors, was moving in and building a high-tech facility. Only the City Planning Commission had any knowledge of the plans and they were all sworn to secrecy. Therefore, everyone in town knew all about it.

The initial office, set quietly between Frozen Expectations Ice Cream Parlor, and Mystique Emporium, maintained its ploy of disguise by decorating its display windows with junk-store relics and black-out curtains as the backdrop to prevent any passing foot traffic from seeing that nothing but cubicles lay beyond. Abbie and the few other employees parked along the alley and came and went discretely through the back door, which added more intrigue and fuel for local gossip. They all knew the townies weren't fooled, the townsfolk were pretty clever, but VEIL'S employees were under orders to remain invisible, so they kept up the façade.

What the townsfolk didn't know was how much Loville, Colorado would grow with the added business and influx of residential needs to accommodate the facility's employment opportunities. Once construction began and the facility became operational, Loville had grown from a population of 1,500 to 4,000 almost overnight.

While a huge corporate construction company built the facility itself, construction workers were suddenly in demand for houses and apartment construction. Downtown boomed with new stores, bakeries, and ethnic restaurants. The movie theater was renovated with three separate screens and fancy reclining chairs. A small RadioShack was soon built just south of town. AT&T and Verizon marked the beginning and end of the downtown strip of businesses. And Apple was negotiating for retail space in the old grocery store that had gone out of business ten years ago. I-HOP, Wendy's, and McDonald's were clamoring for vacant lots along the main road into Loville. Storage facilities popped up all across town. The City Council had to move the city limits to accommodate the new growth.

Abbie had run core-sample analysis those first few months and confirmed the strata was ideal for excavation and construction. A small impact-crater-turned-lake at the foot of the build site was a nice touch. Given the nature of this project and the brilliant people who would be brought to this facility to work, she suggested the Environmental Operations section of her department take advantage of the peaceful beauty of the lake and put tables and seating for ambient mental processing, otherwise known as thinking… and picnics of course. She went so far as to name it QuIET Lake. Quantum Intelligent Entangled Thinking. Seemed appropriate to her.

Abbie blinked, bringing her mind back to the present. The garden groundskeeper had moved to the north quadrant. She seemed to be dividing and transplanting bulbs. Abbie walked quickly through the aboriginal landscape, pausing only after entering the building to scan her badge.

"Morning, Dr. Crossan." The guard, Frank Gonzales, greeted her as he opened a small cubical locker and handed Abbie the key. She put her cellphone in the box and locked the door. Smiling at Frank kindly, she nodded her thanks and rushed through.

The Physics Department was just past the entrance. Hopefully the physicist she most wanted to speak to was in her lab. Dr. Holly Teak had become well known, in the short time she'd been on-site, among those involved in the Quantum Entanglement project because of her extreme ideas. While Abbie knew Dr. Joseph Assad was also on the Physics team, Dr. Teak was less intimidating, albeit irritating. At least Abbie's heart didn't try to win the Kentucky Derby every time she talked to Holly.

Dr. Teak leaned over a laptop along a wall of desk computers, screens, and other machines. Three half empty Lipton tea bottles cluttered the counter. She didn't even move when Abbie walked in.

Abbie scanned the collection of equations on the ceiling-to-floor white board walls that surrounded the lab on three sides. She lifted a contrasting blue dry-erase marker as she walked through the room, studying the equations. Slowly she stepped up to an empty spot, twisted the marker lid off, and wrote out the updated equation. She lifted her tablet, swiped the Tinker Bell graphic to open the digitized duplicate from her smart board, and verified she had the formula written down correctly.

"Holly?" Abbie turned from the 'thinking wall' and cleared her throat. "Uh… Dr. Teak, could I show you something?"

Holly looked up with a heavy sigh, acknowledging Abbie's presence for the first time, then smiled. She looked all of nineteen, but with three PhDs, she had to be at least thirty. "Certainly! What?"

"I was wondering…" Abbie turned back to the board, ran her finger along a troubling quantum formula, and tapped a fingernail on a particular summation. "I have updated the equations with current strata findings, and…

can you show me where the current effects from the strata have been populated in your calculations?"

"Sure!" Holly looked at the equations that Abbie questioned. She tilted her head right, then left, then drew a big red circle around one term with a dry-erase marker. "This term right here" —she tapped the board with the marker, leaving red dots— "could be positive or negative. We shall make the assumption it is positive and thus would have a negligible effect on the process of photon entanglement."

Abbie stared at the scientist in disbelief. First, this chemical physicist had figured out Abbie's equations in less than ten seconds, and second, she immediately dismissed the major influence and Abbie's concerns. "So you're *not* taking into consideration the strength of the resonant fields in the material surrounding our facility? May I ask why not?"

Dr. Teak smiled as if she were speaking to a child who had asked why the sky was blue. Abbie held her temper and let Holly respond.

"Well… though it goes against my nature, we chose to be conservative. We felt that any effect from resonance would only help us. It would create *more* entangled particles. That's what we want! So if it helps, yippee!" She shook with excitement, her fists clenched in front of her like a cheerleader with pompoms.

Yippee? Abbie swallowed, regretting the balsamic

dressing on that Cobb salad at lunch. She had to keep her emotions in check. "But, Holly, I have conducted extensive core sample analysis in this mountain, not to mention seismic— never mind— the bottom line is you may get too much entanglement."

Again Holly tilted her head. She reminded Abbie of her dad's hunting dog, Rex, when Dad blew the seemingly silent dog whistle.

"The more the merrier! We want giga-entanglement. The first time we fire up my crystal, we'll know if we're on the right track. Eventually, we want to go for peda-bits of quantumly entangled particles. Qubits! I love that they are called qubits!"

"Right track? But the strata—"

"—might help us!"

"—might create mathematical instability!" Abbie finished, exasperated.

"And that's good." Holly's perfectly straight teeth glistened.

"No, I mean — look, I may have only minored in Probability and Quantum Mechanics, Holly, but I'm talking about the possibility of a dimensional instability!"

"Ah! String theory. Well, maybe. That could cause us to lose a lot of the entangled particles we create, but the containment team will have the burden of figuring out how to capture the little gremlins once we prove we can create 'em."

Abbie threw up her hands and paced in front of her equations.

Holly smiled. "I know you put a lot of work into finding this place in the mountain. And it's perfect. Really. I love it here. Thank you. And the QuIET Lake is a really nice touch. Great place to have a picnic, or walk, or… to think —"

"Please listen to me, Holly." Abbie wanted to shake her by the shoulders. If this was Patrick or Karole, she would have. "What you're doing is reckless" *—blame the equation, not the scientist*, Abbie chanted in her head the one line she had retained from the Effective Communication with Scientists class that she had been forced to take for her Qual-card— "I'm sorry, but I'd like for you to consider the possibility of cascade effects of VEIL's QUEST on the surrounding quartz strata—"

"Ok. I'll consider it." Holly pursed her lips and furrowed her brow in an over-animated display of either concentration or annoyance, Abbie wasn't sure which. "Nope, I reach the same conclusion. Prolific particle entanglement. So… yay!"

Abbie stepped back, crossing her arms. What else could she say to get through to her? "All I'm saying, Dr. Teak, is if the calculations for the alternate solution to this equation are *not* taken into account, the possibility for effects on our immediate environment— well, the consequences could be" — Abbie swallowed hard— "a catastrophic accident waiting for a place to happen."

Holly stared at Abbie. "The only problem I see is how the containment team is going to herd our little bouncing particles if they make that many that fast."

Abbie frowned. *What if the problem is a horrific event that changes everything as we know it?* But she didn't articulate that thought. Holly was so focused on the positive possibilities, she couldn't see any negative probabilities.

Quantum entanglement was not a toy to be played with. Maybe Holly was right and they would just have a mountain-full of entangled photons. No big deal.

But the other possible results *should* be considered. A great deal of respect and caution had to be incorporated into every theory, hypothesis, formula, and experiment. This was all new territory. She had to make someone understand. Somebody had to listen. But it wouldn't be Dr. Holly Teak. Should she go straight to Director Adam Stettler, the Project Director? Well, she would if she had to. For now, she'd keep trying to get through to the scientists on the Quantum Interim Entanglement Team. Even if she had to wreck any possibility of dating Dr. Assad, she'd risk it, for the sake of the people in Loville.

But hopefully, she didn't have to take that extreme measure. Hopefully everything would go fine and she'd have a chance to get to know the handsome physicist before Holly and her enthusiastic race to entangle photons by the qubits wreaked havoc on the entire state of Colorado.

Maybe Patrick would listen.

As lead programmer with IT in the ops center, overseeing the experiments in the QUEST lab, her brother would have some influence with the team of scientists. Abbie drew her lip into her mouth. She had never been to his area. He had always come to her. The QUEST Operations Center was one of the labs seated back against the mountain. Not above her clearance level, just beyond her scope of practice.

Abbie walked toward the front entry security guard, showed her badge, unlocked the little locker, and retrieved her phone. In the garden she lifted her phone while glancing around for Ling. She was raking leaves in another area of the garden. The garden was lovely with its huge ponderosa pines, aspen clusters, and evergreen shrubs. The aspen leaves were just beginning to turn, like the one she put in her hair this morning. Her brother answered. She turned her back to the gardener for simulated privacy.

"Patrick! I need to talk to you!"

"What is it?" His end sounded muffled as if he'd covered the mouthpiece of his phone. "Keep applying those formulas and we'll run that in a minute, Minerva."

"Is that Minnie? Tell her hi for me."

"Yeah, whatever. What do you want, Abbie?"

She chewed her lower lip. "I need to show you something."

"I'm a little busy... what?"

"I've been concerned about this for a while. I can't seem to get anybody to listen—"

"What are you talking about?"

"I'm going to send you a graphic. Will you look at it, please?" She shouldered her cell phone and lifted her tablet, thumbed past Tinker Bell wielding a wand and opened the copy of her equations from the smart board, then sent it to the secured server where Patrick could open it.

He tsked his tongue in that irritated way. "Just a minute— Okay. So?"

Abbie sighed. "Really look at it, Patrick! I've written it on Dr. Teak's white board too, do you want to come look at it there?"

"What's the problem, Abbie?"

She took a deep, calming breath. "Everybody's so focused on making this gigabyte quantum entanglement work, they're not preparing for the possibility of negative results, *catastrophic* negative results."

"What catastrophic negative results? Abbie, photon entanglement has nothing but positive applications: better communication, quantum computing that practically reads minds. How could there be any catastrophic negative results with that? You're like the old geezer telling Orville that if man were meant to fly, God would have given him wings." He laughed.

"Listen to me!" She squeezed her phone, since he wasn't in front of her. "I'm talking about… instabilities that could cause unknown changes to our world as we know it. I'm just asking you to look at my equations, please give it some merit in the decisions that are being made in there."

Silence pulsed between the phones.

Patrick sighed. "Even if I thought your concerns had merit, Abbie, I'm just an IT guy! Those physicists wouldn't listen to me."

Abbie closed her eyes, releasing a frustrated sigh. She drew in another breath and let it out slowly.

"Abbie." Patrick's tone softened. "I am present during many discussions. From what I overhear, they *are* taking *everything* into consideration. They're using a conservative approach to these experiments. Everything has been within normal tolerance range. I promise. Go back to your cheese sauce department, do your job, and let me do mine. Today we're firing off the whole shebang."

"I know. The full-scale QUEST firing is today!" It took everything inside her to ignore his slam against the acronym for her department. "Why do you think I've come to you with this?" She paced frantically in front of a round concrete table.

"Abbie, I swear, if I see any anomaly, I'll call it out. Go back to your—"

"Patrick! Dr. Teak told me they have *chosen* to ignore the negative probabilities. You can't *ignore* a *probability,* especially a negative one when the equations clearly—"

"Abbie!" A lifetime of sibling squabbling echoed in his voice. "You're just projecting your paranoia onto everybody else's work. Trust us... Trust me! We are not being careless with this! It's too important. And besides, Dr. Teak is brilliant. The toroid crystal is her brain child. She's a genius!"

"Everybody here is a genius, Patrick! Even that groundskeeper is probably a genius!" She pointed at the woman even though her brother couldn't see. "Just because a person is a genius doesn't mean they can't overlook something as obvious as the nose on their face."

Patrick laughed. "Abbie. We *have* taken into consideration everyone's nose and all of the positive and negative results, I promise."

Abbie clenched her teeth. God, he was so stubborn! Just like Mom!

Her brother softened his tone. "Karole told me we're meeting at The Oasis after work. I'll see you there, and we can laugh about how all your fears were unfounded after today's QUEST firing."

She chewed her lip. "I hope so."

"I know so. See you later."

"Wait. What time is the... *whole shebang* gonna be conducted?"

He paused.

Was he considering not telling her? Squinting her eyes in anger, she inhaled to scream at him.

"It's scheduled in three hours."

She nodded to no one. "I'll see you then."

She'd never been to the QUEST lab or the Ops Center, but she had a Quantum, Extra Sensitive Information, Top Secret Clearance. What harm would it cause if she slipped in to watch? At least if things went wrong, she'd be with her brother.

"Abbie! It's a super boring event, honest. There's nothing to see, it's mostly sub-atomic."

"Uh huh," She nodded again. "I know. See you in three hours."

"Abbie—"

She thumbed the icon to disconnect and slipped her phone in her lab coat pocket. Frankly, she hoped her brother and everybody else was right. Her gut told her different.

Chapter Three

Frank Gonzales smiled at Abbie as she approached the Quantum Labs security guard station for the second time in one day. She was thirty minutes early and not in a big hurry this time. "Back again, eh?" His fingers poised over a registry keyboard. "Destination, Dr. Crossan?"

She laid her badge under the scanner. "I'm gonna watch the first full-scale entanglement firing, Frank"

"Ah, Observation Area, Lab One." He typed in the information, and noted the green light accepting her entry. A heavy metal-barred gate snapped open and Abbie pushed through. He locked her phone away and handed her the key. She stared down the long ominous hall.

"Have fun." He turned back to his computer.

"Yeah." She pursed her lips. "And where is that, exactly?"

He turned and pointed with two fingers, reminding Abbie of an airline steward indicating the emergency exits. Would there be a safe exit if this experiment went terribly wrong today?

"Take this hall to QL5, then turn right. Go about twenty yards and you'll see a set of double doors. You'll have to scan your badge to get through, then you turn left. It's… oh, maybe thirty-four yards farther. You'll see a big black cable with a green stripe overhead, that tells you you're heading the right direction. If the cable has a blue stripe you're in the wrong place." He chuckled. "Don't wanna go there."

He continued pointing as if they could see a holographic map in the air. "There's another security station at the end of that hall. Rick Sharp will scan you in. Once you're through that station, you'll want to go right and then left again—"

"I've never been that deep in the Quantum Labs Array."

He stared at her. "Yeah, not many people have… uh…" He scanned the hall behind her. Dr. Joseph Assad, of all people, walked toward them. His red Physics lab coat parted from the breeze generated by his swift pace up the adjoining hall.

Frank held out a hand to stop the physicist. "Ah, Dr. Assad. Are you going anywhere near OAQL1?"

Assad drew his brow in puzzlement.

"As a matter of fact, I am headed to the Observation Area now." He looked at Frank and then Abbie. "Dr. Crossan." He nodded once, a slight smile quivered at the corner of his mouth, as if he knew a secret.

Abbie apprehensively returned his smile. The heat of embarrassment flooded her face. Why had Karole given him Abbie's phone number? It was bad enough that she had dragged her across the cafeteria to talk to him. Abbie's eyes dropped to her shoes. Of all people she'd run into *him* now.

"Perfect." Frank gestured for Abbie to walk toward Assad. She stayed where she was. "Dr. Crossan is going there, too. Could you show her the way?"

Abbie restrained the inner-high-school-girl's gasp that gripped her lungs. "Oh, no," she stammered. "I can wander around until I find it."

"It's no problem." Assad crooned in his smooth-as-silk, sexy hispanic accent.

Her knees went weak. "I-If you're sure."

He held out his hand, inviting her to walk with him. "Jes, I'm chure."

Lord, that accent was going to do her in!

"Thank you, Frank." Abbie bit her lip. Frank was as bad as her sister, forcing her to interact with Dr. Assad.

Frank called out, "You kids have fun!"

This wasn't a prom date! Abbie's face flushed with heat again. Did everybody know she was interested in this gorgeous chemical physicist? It was so much better anonymously admiring him from across the cafeteria. What if it turned out that he hated her? The fantasy would be squashed for good.

She sighed and let him lead the way. Her pale-yellow Environment Department lab coat flapped against his as she walked swiftly to match his long stride. The deeper they went, the tighter the security. The closer to the *whole shebang* in QUEST Lab One they walked, the tighter her stomach clinched.

She had studied this mountain and determined the quartz strata could support the structure of these labs being built against the mountain, like chiseling out a highway. It essentially hid how big the facility truly was by exposing only the front quarter of the structure.

His hand pressed into her back as she crossed the threshold at the double doors Frank had mentioned. A thrill shot through her back and landed in her heart like the impact crater that formed QuIET Lake. She did her best not to squeal or walk on her tip-toes.

"Thank you." She uttered at last.

"No problem-o." He chuckled. "The Ops Center had a pool you might show up for this."

A second wave of heat flushed her face.

"The Ops Center?" She stopped walking. "Who in the Ops Center?"

He hesitated. "Uh, well, Patrick Cros—"

"My brother, Patrick? What did he say?"

Oh, how high school was that question? Why hadn't

Karole minded her own business? This infatuation was so much more fun when Dr. Assad had no idea it existed. Or did he? No. No way. Abbie had never talked to her brother about her feelings for the physicist.

Or had she?

Her bottom lip became the target of her teeth, she bit firmly, trying to remember if she'd ever mentioned anything to Patrick.

Assad looked at her with a twinkle in his beautiful dark eyes. "Nothing. Just— he bet you were concerned enough to probably show up to see that everything went well with this first full scale firing, and I— well, I said you would not come. I mean, it's no fun if no one bets the alternative side—"

"He bet… that I'd… how much did you two bet?"

His smile never faltered. "Just ten dollars."

"Just… ten dollars?" Anger roiled in her gut. "When? When was this? Before we talked in the cafeteria?"

Now seriousness replaced his jovial gleam. "Well… yes. Yesterday, in fact."

Was that why he had been so willing to walk her here? To gloat that he'd won the bet with her brother. No wait, if she showed up, Assad would lose. She clinched her fist at her sides. Would everyone be laughing at her when she walked into the observation area?

Calm down! She stared at the floor. *Breathe!* Drawing

in a long slow breath, she let it go and tried to let the anger go with it. Did she want to expose her *crazy* before their first date? Not that the get-together at The Oasis later was a date, but she really hoped it would lead to one.

That chance may have been ruined if he thought she was a spaz. Her words jumbled up behind her tongue, like a sudden rock slide. She swallowed trying to regain the ability to speak. Should she turn around and go back to her office?

Or continue to Lab One by herself?

But she didn't know the way. This lab array was like a maze. She lifted her chin a notch and continued to walk toward the impending full scale firing. She had every right to be there for the initial event. Humiliation aside, her concern was valid and quantifiable. In truth, she hoped she was wrong. Because if she were right—

Chapter Four

They walked through the second security point. Rick Sharp, indeed, scanned them through. On down into the bowels of the facility they went. At last they came to some stairs that would lead to the observation area above Quantum Lab One.

She dropped her eyes to the steps as they ascended. She and he took each step the same, right, left, right, left, and at the same pace, too. How odd, they seemed synchronized as if they'd come to this lab a thousand times together.

Assad looked across the observation area as they stepped onto the landing. Dimples appeared with his smile.

Oh, man! Could he get any cuter? Her midsection turned to goo. She scanned the room for Patrick. Her brother didn't seem to notice them entering. He had his usual engrossed-concentration stance as he stood behind a computer operator, staring at her screen.

Abbie turned to Dr. Assad. "I'm sorry. Sibling rivalry

and all that."

He glanced past her shoulder and shrugged. Was that for Patrick or her? His warm chocolate eyes returned to hers. "I understand. I have seven sisters and I'm the youngest of eight children. I get… siblings." He smiled a beautiful, white-toothed smile.

Those dimples again! She wanted to palm her forehead, but kept her hands at her side.

"Will you excuse me?" Assad touched her arm lightly and walked toward Sandy East, Test Director.

Abbie watched him walk away. The man had no idea what his touch did to her. Perhaps that was for the better. She rubbed her arm where the sensation still resonated.

Dr. Assad and Ms. East shook hands. He spoke to some of the other Ops Center personnel, including Patrick, and returned to her side. Had he congratulated them on today's achievement or the final outcome of the money pool? She glared at her brother, then turned her gaze to Assad. This interaction between her new friend and her brother was the least of her concerns today.

"I'm hoping for the best here, of course. It's just that— I have concerns, and apparently, I have a different perspective on the equations."

His brow furrowed. "What are your concerns?"

Oh gee. She didn't want to get into a debate with him about this now. Not today. "I could show you… later. I wrote my concerns on Dr. Teak's white board, she circled it with red, no less—"

"Oh. That's what that was."

Abbie stared at him. "You saw… you know what I'm talking about?"

"Well, I noticed the big red circle and I saw the positive-negative possibilities so I mentioned it to Dr. Teak." He paused. "Those were *your* calculations?"

Her knees turned to Jell-o. She held the safety rail that surrounded the top of the stairs. "Yeah. I really wish Dr. Teak would take me seriously. I'm not trying to cause trouble or insinuate negligence. I would just feel better if the effects of the surrounding strata were populated in with the projected outcome in these experiments."

His head tilted in just such a way that he could have been about to say something seductive. Her heart raced out of control, blood pounded against her eardrums. She strained to hear his words.

"We're taking a conservative approach to all of these experiments." His accent warmed Abbie's insides like hot, frothy cocoa. A vision of touching her finger to a dollop of whipped cream on his mouth filled her thoughts. She pulled in a jerky breath. Without thinking about it, her tongue touched the outside of her lip, as if to retrieve the imaginary whipped cream. She focused her mind to hear his words and not his sultry accent.

At least he was *listening* to her. Nobody else had given her the slightest never-you-mind. Not even Patrick. She forced a smile and looked up at him. "I know, Holly mentioned it was more conservative than she'd like."

He chuckled. "Yes, that sounds like our Doctor Teak."

Abbie's eyes darted to his. "So… you get… you see why I'm—"

His chuckle erupted into a full-belly laugh. "Don't tell me, let me guess, she told you she's assuming all the potential negatives are positives and thus would have a 'negligible effect on the process of photon entanglement?'"

Abbie's eyes widened. "That's word-for-word what she said."

He stepped beyond the protective guardrail at the stairs and gestured for her to enter the front half of the Ops Center designated for observation and surveillance. Several people were seated at computers in front of the windows that overlooked the huge laboratory. The lab below was so big it could double for a gymnasium if the need ever arose. Quantum Entanglement Basketball. Abbie snorted quietly at her private joke.

She spotted Minerva Wong by her short black hair and small Asian stature at one of the terminals and walked up behind her. Patrick had dated her several months ago, but they didn't work out. Abbie and she had remained friends, nonetheless. "Hey, Minnie."

"Oh hey, Abbie." A quivering smile lifted the edge of Minnie's mouth. How much had she put into the Ops-Center pool?

Peering over Minnie into the lab below, Abbie folded her arms across her ribs. "Big day, huh?"

Minnie nodded.

Abbie wanted to see as much of the lab as possible. She positioned herself at a spot centered with the Quantum Entanglement Symmetrical Toroid anchored directly below the windows. It was amazing how huge the QUEST was. Abbie's Subaru could drop down through the center of that thing and never touch a single component. What a *quest* it was to achieve this level of quantum entanglement. It truly was an exciting achievement, if it worked right and didn't blow them all into outer space… or something crazy like that.

Angling herself for an optimal vantage point felt morbid, like positioning herself for a better view of a car wreck. Guilt riveted her heart for such pessimistic thoughts. She wanted to be more positive about this experiment. She hated being the empty tomb, but so far she couldn't find anybody who was taking her concerns seriously. Except possibly Dr. Assad. Or was he just humoring her?

She looked around the observation area. A gnawing sensation tightened her stomach more. Should she even be here? Nausea lapped at the back of her tongue. There were no extra chairs to pull over. She'd made such a production of being here, she *had* to stay now. See it through. She glanced at Patrick and the others at the back of the room. No one appeared to be concerned for their lives.

Several scientists stood around her. It was like standing in a mosh pit at a concert, only instead of large, loud speakers, they were facing computers and observation windows overlooking the most unique piece of equipment on Earth. Smiles and jovial conversations hummed among them.

Assad stood next to her. "I know what you are saying. Doctor Teak and I have had that same discussion many times."

She stamped down her fears. He really was listening. "You have?"

"Sure."

As Abbie breathed a small sigh of relief, his cologne pleasantly permeated her awareness. Most scientists smelled… sterile. What did he wear? Ralph Lauren? Dior? She didn't dare ask. Without turning to face him, she asked a more appropriate question. One which also lurked in her mind.

"I suppose it won't be much of a spectacle. Just some glowing lasers and computer read outs counting a small percentage of the photons that become entangled?" A nervous giggle erupted from her lips. Where did that school-girl chortle come from?

"Not even that. The lasers are beyond the scope of human vision. All that we expect is to watch the crystal take on a glow. I predict it to be an interesting *spectacle*, as you say. Like a diamond with bright lights shining through its facets." He chuckled. "A five gallon bucket-sized diamond."

She giggled again. "Yeah, that crystal is something else. I guess it's a blatant example of Teak's genius."

"True. It is her— I don't know how to say it in English — brain baby. Is that right?" He saddled up next to Abbie. "Do you mind if I stand with you?"

She resisted the 'Pfffft!' that popped in her head and calmly responded, "No. I don't mind." Her eyes met his. For a moment she was lost in the chocolate depths. "Uh. Brain child, I think you're trying to say."

He nodded with a mischievous smile. Was he teasing her about his limited knowledge of English colloquialisms?

Footsteps echoed in the stairwell. Dr. Teak popped into the observation area. Two other scientists were close behind her.

"Dr. Teak." Assad greeted Holly with little emotion. A professional air of neutrality hung in the room.

Abbie tore her eyes from Joseph. Holly seemed to ignore everyone. Her focus directed to peruse the computer screens, reading the information each one displayed. She settled in front of an observation window above the young assistant on the lab floor, who waited behind a plexiglass shield. He wore a red t-shirt. Abbie squinted to make out the words.

Never trust

an Atom

They make up

everything!

Abbie chuckled. "That's cute."

A man in a mechanics-brown lab coat circled the toroid and joined the assistant behind the shield. Abbie knew his face but not his name. She swung her attention to Holly who leaned over Minerva to look directly down at the QUEST and waved when the Chief Technician lifted his eyes. Holly's fingers rolled in succession, once again reminding Abbie of a middle-school girl waving to a boy in a concession stand.

"Huh?" Abbie looked down. Did they have something going on between them? She shrugged and brought her attention back to the school-bus-sized machine surrounding the brilliantly designed crystal. Dr. Teak's genius could not be denied.

Abbie drew her gaze back to the computer terminals in front of her. Data scrolled up the screen as Minnie and her team gazed intently at the numbers. The windows overlooking the lab had been polished recently. Why that caught Abbie's attention, she had no idea, but the glass was so clean it was practically invisible. Two more scientists, entered and stood to Abbie's left.

Almost everyone spoke in hushed tones. The environment in the Ops Center lent itself to speaking quietly, like a library or a funeral. But Holly Teak's voice rose above the general hush. She sounded and acted like a younger-than-average straight-A-student at the district-wide science fair, who knew beyond a shadow of a doubt she was going to win. She always won. Why would today be any different?

A sensation slammed into Abbie's gut like she'd swallowed stones. She shouldn't be here! She closed her eyes and said a small prayer. *Please let me be wrong*!

A speaker squeaked as Sandy East, Test Director, tried out the sound system. "Testing, one, two, testing. Is the sound okay? Alright."

Abbie turned to look through a clear-screen computer monitor, the size of a large white board, that served as a divider between the Operations Center and the observation area. Ms. East stood among the rows of computers and technicians at the back where Abbie's brother stood with his arms folded across his chest. He winked at her. Butterflies of concern fluttered in her gut, but her brother's jovial wink helped ease her worry. The huge, clear screen received Sandy's system check verifications. It read backward to Abbie.

Patrick paced the Ops Center the way he did when he was working out a difficult programing problem. And he looked agitated. Was it the numbers scrolling before him that concerned him, or her presence? Abbie drew in a deep breath and let it out slowly. All of the Ops Center personnel at the back would watch the QUEST firing results from their computer screens.

Abbie craned her neck to look into the lab below. The man in the brown lab coat walked around the toroid again. Her eyes remained on the man below, as she spoke softly to the scientist at her side, "Doctor Assad, who are those guys on the lab floor?"

He lifted his gaze to her. "I prefer you call me Joseph."

She nodded. "Joseph. Who are they?"

"That's Axel Ashton. He's the best tech I've ever worked with. The man can put together any fantastical design we physicists come up with. I think that's why he and… a certain scientist"— he inclined his head toward Dr. Teak— "get along so well. Whatever we dream up, he builds. And the kid in the red t-shirt is Zeke Callahan. I understand he just got engaged, last night."

"Really? Huh? Okay, but why are they on the floor with the QUEST?"

"There's 1,024 lasers in that circular machine precisely directed at that crystal. I believe he manually set every one of them to her prescribed specifications." He glanced at Dr. Teak who remained engaged in her chatty, effervescent, hair-tossing conversation. "I suppose he's there to ensure they stay aligned, you know, in case any of them need readjusting." Joseph shrugged. "Or yell 'abort' if anything goes wrong in that donut."

A shiver ran over Abbie's spine. She glanced at the stairs. How far could she get, really? Returning her eyes to Mr. Ashton, she nodded. "A donut the size of a school bus, designed to produce quantum-bits of entangled particles. What could go wrong?"

She lifted worried eyes to meet his. His tongue slipped across his lips in amusement as he gestured agreement. Abbie stared at his mouth. Suddenly her mind focused in wonder. What would it feel like to kiss those lips? Soft, inviting, and with that sultry accent, she imagined his kiss to be… intoxicating.

Mentally, she shook her head and forced her eyes at the activity on the floor. Was it suddenly hot in here? She adjusted her arms to air out the wet coves. *Secret, don't fail me now!* She wriggled in the spot where she stood.

"Are you alright? Would you like me to find you a chair?"

"No. I think I can see better if I stand."

Joseph laughed. "There's really not much to see. It's mostly—"

"Sub-atomic, I know." She laughed with him. "Still, I want to watch."

What a blatant contrast to the anxiety that had been brewing in her gut over the effects of this experiment. Here she was laughing and flirting like this experiment was a routine walk in the park. Guilt squeezed her heart like a vise. She sobered and cast her eyes on the activity below. The moment of truth was at hand.

This flirting could wait for later at The Oasis. If everything went okay in the next few minutes. Maybe she should have just waited at the bar to hear how the experiment went. She let her eyes land on the stairwell, imagining herself sitting at a cocktail table for people she hoped would show, waiting endlessly because everything went wrong. She swallowed back the anxiety once again. No, better to be here.

The young technician, Zeke, moved around the QUEST with Ashton. He seemed antsier than the Chief Tech. "Are you sure it's safe for them to be on the floor when that thing fires?"

Joseph leaned to speak softly next to her ear. "Positive."

The warmth of his breath sent a ripple of goosebumps down her arm. She resisted the shiver that followed.

Ashton glared at the laser panels as if he expected something to happen. A smile curled on one side of Abbie's mouth. Waiting was the toughest part of any experiment. Patrick had mentioned Ashton was one cool dude, now she knew who he spoke of, and had to agree. He looked very calm for where he was and what he was doing. Certainly calmer then she felt.

Zeke now stood beside Ashton behind the thick shield. It must be time.

"Two minutes to Full-Scale QUEST Firing." Ms. East announced, bringing all discussion to an end in the observation area. Abbie turned to see Sandy staring at the clear screen.

A digital clock on the wall glowed red numbers. The hour, minutes, and seconds displayed as a glaring contrast to the count down. Abbie straightened her back and drew in a ragged breath. Too late to run, she'd barely make it to the first security station if things went bad. She wrapped her arms around her waist and watched the two men below settle behind the Plexiglass shield. *Please let me be wrong.*

"Ninety seconds to ignition, alignment test beams activated…" Sandy spoke in a subdued tone.

Anxiety fluttered in Abbie's gut like a thousand dragonflies. She swallowed bile, pursed her lips, and scanned the room below.

The technicians looked relatively calm. The scientists

at the terminals in the Observation Area looked calm. Minnie looked calm. Sandy East, of course, sounded calm. She had the perfect voice to announce the count down. She could easily record one of those meditation tapes, her voice had that soothing, tranquilizing quality to it. If only listening to her count down the execution of this experiment would settle Abbie's pins-and-needles nerves right now.

"Alignment nominal. Checking capacitor power levels…" Ms. East's voice flowed from the speakers like syrup.

Axel lurched as if he were going to do something beyond the shield, then he settled in place. Abbie's inside lurched too. What was that about?

"Capacitor power levels all within safe parameters. Checking crystal optics…" Ms. East's voice echoed slightly.

Abbie scraped her top teeth across her bottom lip, still clinging to herself as if she were cold. She glanced at the clock.

"Crystal optics excellent," Sandy cooed. What a gift that voice must be.

Ashton put his arm around Zeke's shoulder. A here-we-go hug? Then stood still beside him. This could be history in the making.

"Quest firing in 30 seconds. Check safety gear and take your positions!"

What position? Crash position, with her head between

her knees? How did Sandy maintain such calm in her voice?

Abbie repositioned her stance. Maybe she should have opted for a chair. If she fainted, she'd never live it down with her sibling.

"Ten." Sandy stated flatly. The clock's seconds flashed forward with the time, yet an eternity passed between number changes. Abbie looked back at her brother, then down at Ashton, and finally at the crystal in the middle of the toroid. If anything went wrong, it'd start in that crystal where all those photons would be splitting.

"Three." Joseph took Abbie's hand and squeezed it. A thousand sensations flooded her mind. Most of them pleasant.

"Two." Abbie drew in a deep breath and held it. Was this what it felt like to stand in front of a firing squad?

"One."

Time stood still… suspended in some alternate reality. Abbie's lungs burned. Her eyes stung. She didn't dare blink. She didn't dare breathe…

"Fire!"

Chapter Five

Nothing happened.

Abbie stared at Axel Ashton. He stared at the crystal. Zeke remained motionless.

Abbie let go and air rushed from her lungs. She glared at the QUEST. A metallic taste in her mouth brought her attention to herself. Had she bit her lip?

She released the assaulted lip from her teeth and swallowed.

Joseph's anxious clamp on her hand lessened. A sigh escaped his lips. "Well, that was—"

Light emanated from the center of the crystal, growing brighter and brighter. Abbie tightened her grip on Joseph's hand. He gently touched her arm with his free hand. "That's expected. In fact, I predicted it. The photons are splitting into our visual range now, that's why it appears to be a white light. But watch, I predict—"

A flood of multi-colored light filled Lab One and the observation area. A rush of fear slammed into Abbie's chest.

Her mouth went dry. She gasped with a jerk backward. Joseph wrapped his arm around her shoulder, "No, it's alright. I predicted this light show, too."

It sparkled like glitter had been thrown in the air. It would have been beautiful if it weren't so alarming. Joseph kept telling her it was what he expected.

But it was what Abbie had expected too, only she expected it to be a bad thing. A catastrophically bad thing.

"That's what we predicted." Holly's loud, arrogant voice penetrated Abbie's fear-saturated mind. Anger festered in Abbie's gut. Fiery eyes darted to Holly, then back to Joseph's calm face.

It's alright. Joseph predicted this. It's not catastrophic.

He nodded in agreement with Holly's statement. Abbie nodded with him, settling her erratic breathing. The pressure lessened in her ears from her heart pounding so hard. Her eyes dropped to the room below. It's alright. She forced a smile, letting relief wash away the worry. It was alright. She panted.

But the light from the crystal continued to swell, filling the rooms. Axel and Zeke moved, taking a step back. Her anxious heart thrummed into an accelerated rhythm again. Regardless of Joseph's insistence that this was predicted, something was not right! Abbie opened her mouth, "What's wro—?"

An explosion rocked the room. A thousand rays of

colorful lights radiated from the giant crystal, saturating everything in an instant, like an overexposed negative. Instinctively, Abbie squeezed her eyes as tight as possible, and dropped to the floor.

Burying her face against her arm, she prayed she had closed her eyes in time to protect her eyesight. Something heavy and warm lay across her back. Had the ceiling collapsed?

She dared to lift her head to peek through slitted eyelids. The brilliant light still blanched everything, but, thank God, she could see. The other people were on the floor too, in various huddled positions to protect themselves. Only Holly remained standing.

Just then, the window pane shattered. Abbie hunkered down tighter, covering her head with her arms. The weight pressed harder over her back, but the shattered glass did not fall across her as anticipated. A whooshing sound and a stream of wind immediately roared across her toward the lab's back wall. Where had the glass gone? Papers rattled and fluttered past her head. What was happening?

Cautiously she lifted her head. The stream of debris and wind diminished.

Just then the weight pressing on her moved. It was Joseph! He had lain over her, protecting her from whatever had happened. They moved apart and slowly stood. She pulled a curtain of pink hair from her face. The back and side wall of Lab One were gone. Destroyed. But where had the debris gone?

A huge wall of quartz strata stood exposed at the back where the lab was built into the mountain.

Abbie stared at the quartz wall with fear-filled amazement. It glowed and glittered as if fireflies were swarming inside it. "What the—"

She had predicted dimensional instability. Was this that? Good Lord! She buried her face in her hand. What had they done?

Abbie's eyes perused the lab floor. Where was Zeke Callahan?

She scanned the room again. Debris lay scattered across the lab, Axel slowly stood next to the crane, but Callahan— was nowhere. Had he ducked under a desk or something, back where she couldn't see him? Her heart pounded in her ears. She swallowed against a dry throat. "What happened to the kid?"

"I don't—" Joseph's voice faded. Terror filled his face, his eyes fixed on the exposed quartz wall.

"Are you alright?" Abbie looked at Joseph for the first time since she had stood.

The other people moved. First, examining themselves for cuts or blood, then slowly standing, too. Holly looked crumpled on the floor as though she had tried to sit down but the chair had moved away from her and she just fell.

Slowly she climbed to her feet and leaned over the broken window.

Abbie's tear-blurred eyes remained on Holly. She looked enthralled by the chaos below. Abbie wanted to walk over and slap her. But Abbie couldn't move either. Shock had everyone stunned. Anger roiled in Abbie's chest. This was all Holly's fault. Abbie had told that preppy little school girl this experiment could go wrong! She had said the quartz strata needed to be considered and over-producing that much photon entanglement could cause instability—

No. Abbie reconsidered the expression on Holly's face. She didn't look exhilarated by all this… chaos, she looked… stupefied. Did she realize Callahan was missing? Or that Ashton had literally clung to that crane for his life?

God, Abbie hated being right!

Holly stumbled back from the broken window. "My crystal!"

Abbie tore her eyes from Ashton to look at the bent toroid. Abbie gasped! The crystal *was* gone! But so was the assistant!

"What about Callahan?" Joseph said the words, but Abbie's hands balled into fists. If she could reach the woman, she'd punch her in the face. "Is that all you care about?"

Abbie took a step toward Holly, but Joseph blocked her.

"That stupid crystal?" Abbie shouted around his broad shoulder. "What happened to the technician?" Abbie struggled against Joseph. If only she could slap Holly into next Tuesday!

Something filled Holly's eyes— remorse? —fear?

One of the scientists shouted, "Look! Is that… fog?"

Like a mad scientist with some crazy experiment combining dry ice and liquid, a dense fog poured from the exposed mountain strata. Or was it steam? Abbie leaned over the computers. "Axel, get out of there!"

Joseph stared at the mist growing exponentially in the lab. "We have no way of knowing if that's water vapors or poison. It could be hot or cold. It could even be *ácido*… uh, acid!" He turned to the Operations Center.

Project Director Adam Stettler stepped forward. He looked dazed, but decades of military training moved into place with a sobering expression that settled across his face. Joseph hollered at the director. "We need to evacuate this building!"

But no one seemed to hear him. Abbie's eyes widened as she stared at the growing thick mist. If it was hot, it could burn Axel, literally boil him to death right in front of her eyes. If it was acid, he'd dissolve into a puddle of goo. Either way, it would be horrible! He had to get out of there!

Director Stettler lifted a phone. "This is Director Stettler. I'm initiating Emergency Omega Q86." He slammed the phone down. "EVACUATE THIS BUILDING, PEOPLE!"

The vapor oozed over the twisted toroid as the fog crawled across the floor and stretched long fingers up the wall, toward the observation windows.

"This shouldn't have happened!" Holly stammered. "This is terrible!"

Joseph skipped sideways, motioning for the people to move toward the stairs. "¡*Vámonos!* We must evacuate!" He turned to the broken window. "Axel! Get out of the lab!" Then Joseph turned back to the stunned faces standing near him. "¡*Ándale!* Come people, come! Move! Get out of here!"

Stettler did the same with the Ops Center personnel. "Let's go, people! Get out of here!"

The people moved slowly, like cattle, confused and meandering through narrow shoots toward slaughter.

At that moment, the steam, or fog, or whatever it was, oozed over the broken glass. Instantly the fragrance of jasmine, or maybe gardenia blossoms— Abbie sniffed— definitely a hint of orange blossoms, and thick, moist humidity filled the room. But she didn't feel heat. Condensation collected on the panes that had not shattered. Tears of moisture ran down, obscuring the view below. How could fog condensate so fast? This was definitely not ordinary mist.

A strange buzzing sound, Abbie could only think of the South American jungle in Brazil where she'd been on a month-long excavation of a unique outcrop. Could it be a swarm of insects she heard?

She squinted, trying to see through the condensation, then moved to her left to look through the windowless frame. Something huge, but obscured by the fog, lifted from the heavy mist. It hesitated as if pausing to gain its bearings. Lumbersome and thick in its movements, it left the lab through the broken concrete wall. Abbie found her voice. "What on Earth—?"

"I don't think that came from Earth." One of the scientists said with so little emotion Abbie had to turn her head to see if he was in shock or awe. Abbie turned back to the lab, the creature was gone. She spun around to face Holly.

"How's that 'negligible effect on photon entanglement' working for ya now, Dr. Teak?"

Chapter Six

Joseph hurried Abbie into the stairwell. The strange, thick mist hadn't filled the observation area as expected, but hung back as if it had reached its maximum expansion point. Abbie rushed down the stairs. The huge, dark —whatever it had been— that seemed to have crawled out of the sparkling quartz strata, had disappeared through the fog. Surely it didn't literally disappear, like a magic trick, but when she turned back from the scientist, it was gone.

Had it returned to where it came from or had it wandered out where the hole seemed to have blown through the mountain? Oh Lord, was it loose in the facility? Abbie hurried to get outside and check the damage. How far had the explosion reached? Would the lab be exposed to the exterior woods?

Joseph pressed his hand into her back, pushing her through the corridor. Their hurried pace took them in and out of the twirling stream of red emergency lights every twenty feet as they scurried down the tunnel-like hallway. Security checkpoint guards stood on either side of the passage, waving people through like traffic cops. The exodus bottlenecked but continued to press forward. The air grew hot and stale. Fear saturated Abbie's senses, befuddling her mind. She touched her throat, gasping for breath. Joseph pulled her back by her shoulders from the smothering crowd. "It's alright."

He leaned in near to her, forcing her to look into his face. "Abbie. It's alright. You're safe. We can wait for these people to get through and then we'll go."

Minerva plowed into Abbie's back, shoving her into Joseph. He wrapped her arms around Abbie, holding her steady against him. Minnie shrieked, "Oh God! I've gotta get outta here!" She darted around them only to be halted by the mass of people.

Panic slammed into Abbie's heart again. She panted desperately. Stars sparkled in her peripheral. Joseph put his forehead against hers. "Listen to me. *Te tengo. No dejaré que nada te pase. Tu estas seguro conmigo.*"

His silky-smooth voice penetrated her run-away fear. Calm washed over her like warm water. Her lungs slowed. She could breath— no idea what he had said, but its effect was amazing. The clot of people oozed through the gate. Abbie moved forward with Joseph.

Frank, at the building's front guard station, waved people through the vestibule. Both sides of the security check were open for quicker egress. People rushed through and gathered in the garden between the buildings, waiting for further instructions. About a half dozen security guards trotted into the building. Frank calmly but sternly waved them through.

The guard known as Sarge paused for a briefing."What are we up against, Frank."

"Sarge, I don't know!— the stories coming out of QL1 are— unbelievable. All I know for sure is 'use extreme caution.' We don't know what we are dealing with down there."

"It's not down there." Abbie called to them. "It escaped."

Joseph touched her back. "We saw something rather large come out of— somewhere, and it stepped past the damaged wall. We couldn't tell where it went from there."

"What did it look like? A bear? A mule deer? A mountain lion?"

Joseph shook his head. "No. *Es imposible*! Trust me, *es enorme y peligroso*…" He shook his head and cleared his throat.

Frank interpreted Joseph's lapse into Spanish to the sergeant. "It's impossible. He said, 'it was enormous and dangerous.'"

"You'll know when you see it!" Joseph continued. "But listen to me, it's not a bear, or anything you've ever seen in real life!"

"You last saw it in QL1?" Sarge verified.

"Yes. But I'm telling you. I saw it go through the east wall."

The guards nodded and ran down the hall despite Joseph's insistence that the creature was no longer in the lab. He turned to Abbie. "Come on."

They joined the hundreds of other people standing in the garden. It was unclear what they were supposed to do next, yet everyone waited.

"Where is that… thing?" Abbie stared at the east side of the building where the elevation rose with the mountain. The gardener stood dazed. Had she seen the huge thing move into the woods?

"Did you see anything?" Abbie called to her.

She just turned shocked eyes toward Abbie, but said nothing.

The facility had been built into the mountain, if the explosion destroyed the lab wall, exposing the quartz strata, maybe the force had also taken out the side of the mountain. If that were true, that creature might be in the forest.

Abbie pulled Joseph with her, as she hurried to the side of the Quantum Laboratory building. The indigenous garden followed the natural contour of the mountain, rising with the elevation. The front of the building jutted out of the mountain like an outcrop. A forest of natural foliage, aspens, and pines covered the elevated grounds. The excavation line rose at a sharp angle along the side of the building. Fresh dirt scattered the ground and clung in the trees. Could this be from the explosion?

Her professional curiosity overrode her lizard brain's self-preservation. She stumbled but climbed the rising expanse for several yards, following the loosened dirt and unearthed foliage. Finally, she found it. The gaping hole in the mountain. She lifted her eyes to search for the huge creature they had glimpsed in the lab. Nothing, no footprints, no broken tree limbs, no evidence of it going this way could be seen. Yet, the explosion had shoved through the mountain and made a cavernous opening to the outside. A faint smell of the sickly-sweet flowers and humidity lingered in the exposed aperture.

Then she saw it! She froze in place, not daring to get any closer.

Fingers of the strange fog from which they had escaped, with scintillating colors and the aroma of a rainforest, crawled out of the exposed earth like a gargoyle's breath released in the dead of winter.

She turned to Joseph. "Get Security!"

He nodded and patted his pocket for his cell phone. "My phone! It's locked up."

She turned back to the billowing mist. A silvery mass undulated, like a flight of swallows at dusk, just inside the opaque vapor. "What on earth, Joseph! Wait."

Then… voices. Tiny voices, high-pitched and fast, but clear, just inside the fog. "What is that?"

The tiny voices echoed her question. "What is that?"

But then the voices went on to say things that made no sense. "Look at her energy!" "It's beautiful!" "He has it, too." "Look! The energies match." "Yes. It's the same prism stream." "Is she a warrior?" "Should we squash that energy?" "It's not allowed!" "Quick, make mad!" "Yes, make them mad." "Are you sure?" "I want to get closer." "Me too!" "Can we get closer?"

Was the fog toxic? Was Abbie hallucinating from whatever chemical was disbursed from the mist? Just then the silver, glittery mass broke free of the fog and swarmed Abbie.

"We are free!"

Abbie backed away. Would they bite or sting? Were they poisonous like wasps or flying scorpions? She looked back at the fog. Was there anything else coming out of it?

There were a dozen or so dragonflies swarming her head. Fear swamped her senses, and yet she was fascinated. She cocked her head back to get a better look. They didn't seem to be going after her, to sting her. She looked more carefully. They were not bugs.

Tiny… *people* hung gracefully from four iridescent wings like a dragonfly's. The "people" were a little taller than a dragonfly's body, too. Crystal spikes topped their heads like anime hair, and their skin looked… translucent, or iridescent, like rice-paper-thin layers of mother-of-pearl.

They hovered in front of her face. She stared at them, trying to make sense of what she saw. Or what she thought she was seeing. She glanced toward Joseph. Did he see them too?

A delicate, thin cloth wrapped their bodies. Was *that* their clothes? It was opalescent like their wings and flowed around them like a tiny silk sari. Their voices passed smoothly between them like a drifting stream of water.

This had to be delirium.

Abbie turned to Joseph with an uncertain smile. "Are you seeing what I'm seeing?"

His mouth gaped with disbelief. "*¡Sí, Y hablan Español!*"

"What?"

He cleared his throat and dropped his eyes to meet hers. "Do you hear them speaking—?"

"Yes… In English!"

His brow wrinkled over his roman nose. "No, in Spanish!"

They stared at each other. Abbie's head twitched. "You hear them in Spanish?"

"Yes. Don't you?"

"No, I hear them in English. How can this—"

The creatures darted and dove around her eyes, nose,

mouth, and ears. They entangled themselves in her hair, curling themselves in strands of the pink tendrils as if it were strips of cloth. Her smile faded as her breath stifled in her lungs. Fear saturated her mind. She couldn't draw air. She couldn't breathe! They were suffocating her!

Help!

She backed away, tripping over a small brush oak. They swept down with her as she fell, still swarming. She couldn't get away from them. Turning her head from side to side, she struggled to get some distance between her and them. Panic swelled in her chest, like a water balloon filling too fast. Her arms and hands flailed at them, trying to make space for her to breathe. They flew around her hands, landed on her arms, and leapt from her shoulders to her face.

There was no oxygen! Blackness veiled her peripheral. She screamed, "NO!" Crawling backward and thrashing against their attack.

The creatures fell away.

She sucked in air, gasping for the oxygen that had been stolen. Her hand splayed across her sternum, as if that would comfort her desperate lungs. Tears ran down her cheeks.

Her scream had scared them… or something. They flew away from her. All of them seemed startled by her outcry. Then as if a switch had flipped, they fell to the ground. Had she killed them? Perhaps it was they who couldn't breathe in this atmosphere?

Abbie closed her eyes and let the tears flow. Confusion filled her mind. What had happened? What were these creatures? They looked like her beloved Tinker Bell, only they were a shimmery, silvery-white, and Tinker Bell had never terrified her like these creatures had.

But Tinker Bell was a Disney character…

Joseph leaned over her, touching her shoulder and rubbing her back. "That's it. Breathe." He cooed.

"What. Are. They?" Abbie managed to utter.

"I don't know." He leaned away as if to study the creatures writhing on the ground. "Why do they look like they're… hurting?"

"Her pain!" They groaned in a high-pitched sort-of-way. "So much energy!"

Karole's voice from a short distance down the mountain washed over Abbie. "Are you okay?"

Abbie took Joseph's proffered hand to stand. How did anybody know they were here?

A security team trotted a few yards ahead of her sister. They paused near Abbie. "You alright, ma'am?"

Abbie glanced at the creatures writhing on the ground at her feet. Something in her mind indicated she should hide them. She turned back to the guards. Their bullet proof uniforms, their guns at the ready, their big heavy boots, would they stomp the creatures to death and be done with the menace? Quickly nodding, she angled herself to obstruct their view of the winged creatures. "I'm fine. I-I tripped."

"Is this where the explosion came through the mountain?"

Abbie stood between them and the faeries. "I believe so."

"Did you see any… anomalies come out of this hole?"

She forced herself not to look down at the faeries on the ground. "Uh. No."

"Okay. Who are you, ma'am?" The lead officer looked at her badge hanging from her lanyard. He wrote in a small notepad.

She held her badge out for him to get a better look. "Dr. Abbie Crossan, QuESO, I'm environmental."

"Okay. We advise you to clear this area. The auditorium is where everyone will be de-briefed, you should go straight there and let us secure this area." He turned to his team. "Let's set a flag here and see if there are any more explosion sites along this elevation. Hank, you hang back and make sure nothing else comes outta this hole."

"Officer. I'm the geologist for VEIL, I'd like to examine this site, if you don't mind." She held up her hands. "I promise I'll scream if any anomalies come at me."

"Well, I— alright. We'll check up here a little ways and be back to secure this area. Make it quick, Dr. Crossan."

"Yes Sir."

The security team scurried up the mountain.

Abbie angled her head to see her sister still climbing toward her, medical bag in hand. Abbie's panic drained with her sister's presence.

Karole's eyes leveled on Abbie, scanned her face, and swept down to her feet. "What happened? You've got cuts and bruises." She turned to Joseph. "You too."

Karole touched the areas of concern on Abbie's face. Then she spotted the dozen or so creatures rolling over to their hands and knees on the ground, slowly recovering from whatever had happened to them. "What… in… the… world?"

She knelt next to them, sliding an examination glove over her hand and gingerly lifting one in her palm.

The creature struggled, terror obvious in its every movement, then it settled down and gazed at Karole. It was as if fear waned to curiosity. The others continued to rise to their feet, recovering from whatever overwhelmed them a moment ago. They watched their comrade being lifted away from them. One bent its knees, its wings twitched out taut and it sprang into flight, following Karole's hand. The others joined the one and the swarm hovered just inches beyond Karole's palm. She turned to Abbie with wide, fascinated eyes. "Where'd they come from?"

Abbie pointed to the fog. "There was an explosion, or implosion really, and this fog—!" She swallowed. "I was right. Lord help us all, I was right." Huge tears pooled and then spilled down her cheeks.

Karole looked at the creature in her hand. "You mean to tell me, this *creature* came from that fog? But— how?" She assessed what she held. "You don't mean to tell me they came from— as a result of the entanglement experiment?"

Abbie shrugged. "I-I don't know, yet."

Her sister turned back to the swarm, taking in each one. "They— they look like faeries."

Abbie nodded. Her sister was right, but she still was unsure what they were. The one in Karole's hand looked worried. Abbie almost felt sorry for it.

"They… tried to suffocate me." Tears spilt down Abbie's cheeks.

The creature on Karole's palm vehemently shook its head. "Not suffocate. Fascinate!" Then it furrowed its brow and glared at Karole.

Karole turned to Abbie with an irritated roll of her eyes. "Oh, you're just having one of your panic attacks. Look at this!" She held her palm out to Abbie. "Look how cute this is."

Voices rose from the swarm, like a breeze. "She doesn't have that energy." "No, she doesn't." "How fascinating!" "Her energy is different." "What is that?" "I don't know." "It feels like… something different." "I know what this is!" One bobbed in the stream of the swarm.

"Attraction threads?" "Look, their lining up! "Oh, but look at this one." The swarm swung over to Joseph. "Yes." "This is the one." "He has the same prism stream." "The same attraction threads." "Remarkable!" "Squash it, before Mother Righteous finds out." "No, wait!"

Karole smiled at the one now standing on her palm. It looked at its feet and then bounced, as if testing the effect of the tight glove stretched across her palm. Karole grinned wider. "What are you?" Karole barely breathed the question.

The swarm halted several inches from Karole's face. Collectively they spoke, "Crystal Faeries."

The one on her palm bounced from her glove and flew to the swarm. It hovered in front of the swarm. "What are you?"

Karole laughed. "Well, I guess… I'm a human."

"Human!" They all seemed to say various versions of the word. "You look like Mother Righteous when she—" "But kinder." "Yes. Mother Righteous has your eyes." "Not her hair." "No, not her hair."

Like a ribbon, they swung over to Abbie. She ducked back from them as they halted several inches from her face. One slowly flew closer and reached out to take a handful of Abbie's tear. The drop looked to be the size of a cantaloupe in its small palm. It sniffed the ball and lifted its tiny, yet disproportionally large sapphire eyes to meet Abbie's.

She marveled at how beautiful its eyes were, like a

polished jewel.

"Your energy is… amazing." It blinked. Tiny crystals clung to its lashes "Why does it make you leak sea water?"

Abbie stared at the curious faerie. "You-you nearly smothered me. I couldn't breathe."

The faerie let the ball of tear fall from her hand. "We did not mean to… smothered… you. We were… flying to our trees, when a loud noise… Boom!" The faeries flittered around each other. "A lot of… strange things we had never seen before were thrown at us. We ducked behind the big leaves. Then we heard… you. Many of you yelling and running. We were fascinated. Your energy glowed. We could see it from our side. We have never seen this type of energy before. There are stories told…" The lone faerie turned to the swarm, gestured to the woods around them. "Could this be where our stories came from?"

Joseph tapped Abbie's arm but stared at the creatures. "They're speaking English now."

Abbie glanced at him and back to the one who seemed to be brave enough to talk directly to her.

The swarm collectively shrugged, expressing one response. "We don't know—" then their voices separated. "…where the stories came from." "Could it be?" "Mother Righteous lived *here* long ago?"

Abbie leaned closer to the one who seemed to hover in front of the others. "How did you get here?"

"Flew toward your energy." The brave little faerie said as it flew closer to Abbie's hair and took several strands into its hand. It let the strands glide along its palm, as if fascinated with the texture. It sniffed her hair. "Fruit, no… berries?"

"Mixed berries, actually," Abbie answered. "It's my shampoo." Abbie's initial fear had slipped away. Perhaps they were harmless, like her beloved Tinker Bell. She watched from the outer reaches of her peripheral to see what the faerie did. "Are you really faeries?"

The one at her hair stopped and looked directly into Abbie's eyes. "Of course. Crystal Faeries. Are you really human?"

A cluster of faeries seemed to focus their attention on Joseph. That same furrowed brow and squinted eyes. Were they studying him?

Joseph huffed, but it sounded like a short chuckle. "This is amazing. Take a picture! We need a recording of this." He patted his pockets for his phone. Disappointment ebbed his face.

Abbie chuckled and turned back to the faerie. "My name's Abbie. What's yours?"

The faerie stiffened, her wings flapped so fast behind her shoulders that Abbie could barely see more than a blur. "What do you mean?"

Abbie paused. "How are you called?"

The faerie tilted her head, as if considering Abbie's words.

"What distinguishes you from the others?"

"Oh!" The faerie flew backward a short distance. A squeaky-high pitch emanated from her mouth, something like rocks being rubbed on a slate. Abbie cringed. The faerie silenced and stared at her. "You did not understand?"

"I guess not."

The faerie considered Abbie. "You have not our language, but somehow we have yours… hum, curious."

"I hear you speaking English, my native tongue. But Joseph heard you in Spanish, his native tongue."

He touched Abbie's arm and stepped up closer. "No. At first I heard them speaking Spanish in my head, now I hear English when they speak out loud. How can that be?"

"Hmm" The faerie touched her chin. "When we speak among our minds, you hear us in your native 'tongue,' as you say." She seemed to consider that, then opened her tiny mouth. "What distinguishes me from the others is— Aura." She bowed at the waist while her wings buzzed behind her.

"Aura." Abbie smiled. "Please to meet you, Aura. This is my sister Karole with a K and an E at the end."

Karole nodded with grave uncertainty. "Hi."

Aura smiled. "Hello Karole with a K and an E at the end." She turned to the swarm, "Such a long distinction." She shrugged and held up her hand to the other faeries.

"This is my sister Diamond, Amethyst, Jasper, Heliodor, Agate, Malachite, Celest, Azur, Charo, Lole, Emerald, Garnet, Xan, Jade, Kyan, and Morganite."

Abbie chuckled. "You're all named after crystals."

They all stared at her, blinked as if on cue, and then nodded as one. "Yes. We are Crystal Faeries."

"This is so cool!" Abbie glanced at her sister. "But please forgive me if I cannot remember which of you is who. You all look alike to me."

Aura turned to gaze at Karole, then turned back to Abbie. "You look alike to us."

All the faeries laughed. Abbie couldn't help but laugh too.

"Except for the energy," one finally said. "Yes, this is true." "We have not seen this energy." "It is what makes you look *not* alike." "Except him." One pointed at Joseph.

His eyes widened.

"Oh, yes." "His energy matches…" The swarm swung toward Abbie. "You!"

Abbie's eyes bulged. "Me?"

The swarm nodded enthusiastically. "Yes. You." "Don't let Mother Righteous know!" "She would be very angry." "At us." "And you." "She demands it." "We must squash such emotions when she's angry." "We want to stop squashing beautiful emotions." "But she is very strong." "Yes, we must do what she commands." "She sends the shade!" "Or the golem!" They all nodded in fearful agreement.

Abbie's brow furrowed, dipping low over her eye. "What are you talking about? Who is this mother righteous?"

Aura separated from the swarm, flying closer to Abbie's face. "Mother Righteous lives high in the floating mountain."

She serpentined her arms together and lifted one shoulder to her jaw. Her eyelashes fluttered. "But you. You have an energy that Mother Righteous won't allow. And it is the same prism stream as his." She poked one slender finger toward Joseph.

"What does that mean?" Abbie glanced at Karole, then Joseph.

The faeries chortled. As one, they spoke, "Love!"

Some of the faeries swarmed Joseph. A frown replaced their sweet smile. They squinted, as if focusing on him. A harsh sensation seemed to emanate from them.

"An attraction thread." Aura said at last, drawing Abbie's attention back to the leader.

Abbie's mouth gaped. "What? I— we just met! We're not—"

The faeries in Joseph's face squinted. His face flushed, as if he were holding his breath. Fear, or was it anger, washed over his expression.

"That's enough!" Joseph swatted at the creatures.

They scattered out of his reach. Why did they look pleased with his reaction?

"Look. I don't know how you're doing this." He glanced at the hole in the ground, then back to Abbie. "Is this some elaborate joke? Am I being punked? I'm not finding it funny." His hand plunged into his dark curls. "We evacuated the building for God's sake!"

A darkness filled his face. He squinted, glaring at Abbie. "I think I've had enough of your idea of fun. I'm going back to my lab." He stomped away, letting the slope of the mountain affect his momentum.

Abbie turned to her sister, utterly confused. The faeries swarmed her hair. Others moved with her eyelashes as she blinked. "How could he think *I* had anything to do with *this*?" She gestured to the swarm. Then took a double take at the ones in her peripheral.

Karole touched Abbie's arm. "Work Force Development."

Abbie stared at her sister. "What?"

"WFD, on the canisters, it stands for Work Force Development. The joke it that it creates jobs for those who didn't go to college. It's no big deal, and I don't know why I thought it was such a huge secret." She perused the swarm of faeries. "This! Is a huge deal, and we've gotta keep it a secret. Let's get outta here before that security team comes back."

Abbie watched the odd little cluster. Why were they still glaring after Joseph?

Chapter Seven

"I want you to come to medical," Karole touched Abbie's shoulder as they tramped down the mountain.

Abbie focused on the faeries buzzing around her head, like bees to a flower. They seemed harmless enough, a nuisance maybe, but harmless. But something deep in Abbie's gut told her to be wary. Joseph had suddenly become angry and paranoid. Did the faeries have something to do with his sudden change? They had said their dictator forced them to squash emotions that made her angry. Is that what happened to Joseph?

They chattered on and on about her energy and his too. And how Karole's energy was different and the one they called Mother Righteous. They spoke the forbidden "L" word.

Even in their world it was forbidden. But to a much different degree than here. Here it was an etiquette issue. Nobody used the L word so soon after meeting. Abbie wasn't *in love* with Joseph. Lust maybe. Big time attraction, by all means. But how could she even begin to entertain the idea that she had any type of *love* for him?

Why had the faeries said *that*? Just blatantly blurted it out. If their mother righteous banned the emotion, then they had no idea how sacred the word was. Not to be thrown around so flippantly.

Their world?

Where were they from?

Was Abbie right about the quantum entanglement going wrong? Had the explosion caused dimensional instability? Opened up a portal? Was it still open? Would more faeries come through? Was the mist the portal? The faeries said they could see us through whatever happened on their side. A big boom. Debris flew through.

Debris… flew… through— "Aura." Abbie stopped abruptly.

The faeries fluttered about Abbie's head. "Did you see a… a man in a red shirt come through after you heard the big boom?"

The faeries stared at Abbie, blinking as one. "No."

Disappointment filled her heart. She ached to go examine the lab and the quartz wall. She turned to her sister. "Why do I need to go to medical?"

Abbie continued walking, adjusting her vision from the faeries to her sister. Karole held her glasses up off her nose in order to view the flying creatures through her bifocals.

"*You* don't. But I want to take a better look at these little guys and they seem to be attached to you, so… I need *you* to come to Medical."

"You mean you want to… put them under a microscope and… analyze them?" Why did the thought of Karole examining them put such terror in Abbie's gut?

Karole brought her gaze to meet Abbie's. "Well, they are amazing. Don't you want to know more about them?"

Abbie's face washed with incredulous shock. "Yeah, but I thought I'd just talk to them, observe them. This is no different than any other discovery we make in our work. You wouldn't destroy a new form of life you found. You'd look more closely, watch how it functions…" Abbie gasped. "Were you going to" —she lowered his voice to a whisper— "dissect them?"

The swarm gasped and swooped back away from Karole. "She wants to cut us up!" "She wants to kill us!" "She is evil!" "She is like Mother Righteous!"

They crowded Abbie's head. Some landed on her shoulders, in her hair, others flew just inches above her. "Do not let her squash us!" "We want to be with you!" "We want to *know* your love energy." "We do not have to *dissect* you to *study* your energy."

Abbie pursed her lips, stifling her need to shoo them from her personal space. They were scared and sought her for protection. Of course, she would not let Karole, or anybody else for that matter, turn them into lab experiments. These creatures had a voice. They could convey their thoughts. She, too, was very curious to learn more about them, but she'd do so by talking to them, asking questions, exchanging ideas and information, the way one would do when one first met a person. The way she had hoped to learn more about Joseph.

These creatures were persons. Very small, but obviously intelligent, persons. She backed away from her sister. "We do not need to go to Medical, Karole. We are not injured. I'm going to take these faeries to my office and sit down and have a conversation with them. If you want to come ask questions, you're welcome to join us. But if you're thinking of dissecting even one of them, forget it."

Karole frowned. "What's this 'we' business. I… was just thinking of holding a magnifying glass up to them, so I could see them better! I wasn't going to *dissect* anything." She paused, perusing the swarm. "But… if any of them die, you let me know. I *would* like to perform a necropsy!"

"Oh my God! They are quite alive and well. Back off!"

"See, that's another thing… how do you know *they* are well?" She stared at Abbie.

Abbie's shoulders rounded and she continued down the mountain.

"Just promise me, if anything happens to one of them,

you'll save the body—"

Abbie spun around to face her sister. "Karole! Seriously! Back off!"

The faeries flutter above Abbie's head, all glaring hatefully toward Karole. Abbie focused on the ones she could see in her visual range. "Let's go to my office. You'll be safe there. And I have some crystal core samples you might enjoy seeing."

Excitement flitted among them.

"Hey!" Karole called after her. "Don't forget you've got a date at The Oasis this evening."

"What?" Abbie halted. Her mind was so consumed with this phenomenon of faeries she'd forgotten all about the 'gathering of friends'. "With Assad? You saw him storm away, right? I don't imagine he'll be joining us for a drink tonight, or ever." Abbie turned to continue walking, but turned back. "You really think people are going to gather at The Oasis after that… accident?"

"Only makes sense." Karole shrugged. "Trauma, alcohol— kinda goes hand in hand. Besides, I wouldn't be so sure he'll stay angry."

Abbie turned a questioning gaze toward her sister. How would she know what he would do?

Aura swung into Abbie's visual range. "Abbie. He has your love energy. You are matched. He will be there. He wants to be with you." The little faerie turned a disappointed glare to some of the faeries over her shoulder. "We are sorry we pushed anger on him. It is what we do." Aura shrugged. "Mother Righteous demands it. But… we prefer the way it is here."

Another faerie flew up next to Aura, giggling. "It is funny."

Aura turned to her "No, Amethyst! It is different here. You saw! They have love. We can *learn* love here. It's not like Velona."

The other faeries bent their heads. "Yes. Not like Velona." "Will Mother Righteous punish us?" "I do not want to be stripped into nothing but light." "Like the shade."

"Velona?" Abbie focused on them. "Is that where you are from?"

Aura nodded toward Abbie, then touched the other faerie's shoulder. "We do not know what *here* is, but I do not *feel* Mother Righteous's energy. Maybe here we are safe from her. She will not make us suffer… like the shade."

"What is a shade?" Abbie visualized a lamp shade. That's couldn't be right.

The faeries shivered. But none seemed to know how to explain. "Anak was whole, now he is… not."

Abbie tried another angle. "You are afraid of this mother righteous?"

"Not afraid!" Aura stiffened as if offended.

"We stay away." "When she comes down." "From her mountain."

Aura glared at the other faeries's interruptions. "But her energy reaches everyone."

"Huh?" Abbie continued to walk down the mountainside. The faeries swarmed her as she went. "Let's sit down and talk. Do you eat? Do you want water or tea? How do you sustain yourselves?"

"See!" Karole interjected from behind. Abbie had almost forgotten she was still walking with them. "That's something I'd like to know. That's a medical question!"

They buzzed with excitement, chattering about things Abbie didn't understand. She hoped she could at the very least figure out nutrients for them. As fast as their wings flapped, surely they had some system of sustaining that energy. Other than *feeling* her "love energy."

If they survived by absorbing her love energy, they would indeed starve to death. She chuckled at the thought.

Sadness washed over her. She really didn't want them to die. As irritating as it was to have them swarm her face and hair, she was quickly becoming attached to them and wanted to learn so much more. Perhaps find out more about all this love energy and Dr. Assad having a matching prism stream?

Abbie gritted her teeth, fighting the knee-jerk sensation to swat the faeries from her hair and face. They rode on her rather than fly along with her as she made her way to her office. Hiding in her hair and clothes seemed better once she reached her building. A few people moved about the halls. Karole was right about one thing, she should keep the faeries a secret.

Nearly everyone had gone to the auditorium. Karole told Abbie about the facility-wide meeting Karole had ignored when she realized security was called to look for the missing technician from Lab One. "If there was a possibility of finding Zeke Callahan, my Hippocratic oath takes precedence over a schmoozing mandatory meeting to tell everyone that nothing happened. Right?" Karole insisted.

Abbie agreed, but she had a more pressing distraction with the faeries crawling through her hair. The memory of a documentary she had seen a while back played in her head.

A wild dog of some sort, jackals perhaps, had a dominant alpha female and an omega female. Miss Alpha stopped nursing her pups because they had sharp teeth, so the pups went to the omega female and nursed on her. The documentary observers zoomed in on Omega's face. She gritted her teeth and whined as the pups nursed, while the alpha female stood near, daring her to not feed the pups.

That was how Abbie felt about these faeries' fascination with her. They had a right to learn about her. She wanted to learn about them. She just wished they weren't so obnoxiously entangled in her hair and playing with her eyelashes. One sat in her ear. Her wings tickled.

She shivered. "I can't take that! Please don't get in my ear!"

The one that had been in her ear swooped away but came right back and buried herself in strands of Abbie's hair. Abbie sighed. At least it was better than before. She walked swiftly through her building, her sister at her side, and finally reached the sanctity of her office-lab. "Here. This is my office. You'll be safe here."

She collapsed in her chair. "This is my desk. Can you all come here to my desk top" —she patted it— "and let me have a good look at you?"

They complied. Aura led the way in flight to delicately land toe first on the calendar blotter. Abbie marveled at how gracefully they moved, like a skilled ballerina. Aura faced Abbie and waited for the others to join her. Abbie fervently rubbed her scalp. A moaned escaped her lips.

"Now." Abbie pulled out a magnifying glass from a drawer and lifted it to her face. "Let's have a look."

Aura giggled. Karole pressed over Abbie's shoulder to see through the glass too. Abbie shoved her back. She'd seriously had enough of being crowded today. "Give me a minute."

Karole frowned but stood back. The faerie turned

slowly as if looking at themselves in a mirror. Some struck poses like a run-way model and then turned. Abbie chuckled

The creatures were amazing. Fully formed human-like bodies, but where a human's shoulder blades are, they had wings. Four opalescent wings to be exact. They looked so delicate. As if any amount of pressure would crumble their wings or crush their bodies. Something about them all seemed feminine. "Are you all female?"

They smiled and turned their heads toward Aura. She seemed to consider Abbie's question. "Yes. We are like you."

"Do you have males?"

The faeries held their midsections and laughed. Aura glared at her sisters. They controlled their humor and stood attentive. Aura turned back to Abbie's huge eye in the big round glass."Of course! But they are few."

Abbie turned to her sister. "Hmm, makes me think of a beehive, mostly females and a few drones for breeding and…" Abbie turned to the faeries. "What do your males do?"

Again the faeries giggled. Were they embarrassed or laughing at her ignorance? Aura stepped forward. "Our males work hard. They forage for food. They are strong and brave, and they—"

Aura seemed to be searching for the right word. "They serve Mother Righteous, and when we need more faeries, they, well… they breed with our faerie queen." She lowered her voice. "Oh, but we don't call her Queen!"

Abbie turned to her sister again, "See? Like bees. Isn't that fascinating?"

Karole leaned close to them. "Are you hungry? What do you eat?"

Aura turned toward Karole with a frown. Karole gestured putting food in her mouth. The faeries just stared at her with big eyes and open mouths.

"I'm googling it." Karole snatched out her phone.

"WHAT?" Abbie cocked her head back. "You think anything you find on Google is going to be accurate! Faeries are a myth!"

The faeries gasped.

Abbie crunched her face. "No offense… but in our world, you're a myth."

Aura hovered just inches from Abbie's face. "In our world love is a myth."

Abbie stared at Aura. "You have a point. But still…"

Karole pointed at her cell phone. "According to fairy folklore experts, 'fairies prefer natural foods, with pixie pears and mallow fruits being their favorites. Fairies love foods that are sweet and are prepared with… *saffron*. Among fairies' favorite foods are milk with honey, plain milk, sweet butter, and honey cakes.'"

Aura nodded and landed next to her sisters on the desk

blotter. "Crystalized honey is the best. Diamond eats it all the time."

One of the faeries nodded.

Ah, Abbie considered her, that one must be Diamond. She stood a few millimeters taller than Aura. And her crystalized hair seemed more purple. Aura had more of a blue tint to her crystal spikes.

"Amethyst prefers saffron on *everything*." Another faerie coyly dipped her head toward her shoulder and drug her toe across the blotter.

Ah, she's Amethyst. She was shorter than Aura and maybe a little rounder. Amethyst suited her for a name, her crystal-like hair reflected that pinkish-purple hue.

"I can't believe Google is accurate. This is crazy." Abbie observed the subtle differences between the faeries. If she looked long enough, she could see distinctions. She turned to her sister. "Does this mean… our worlds have… somehow they've been here… before?"

Karole shrugged and continued her assessment.

"So high-energy type foods?" Karole remained pressed in close. Abbie elbowed her, moving her away from the faeries, but Karole shoved her back, determined to see them. Abbie sighed and handed her sister the magnifying glass.

Leaning back in her chair, Abbie crossed her arms over her chest. "Why did you *press* angry emotions at Joseph?"

Aura shrugged. "It is what we do."

Diamond flutter beside Aura. "We have to."

Amethyst sprang from the desk top. "Mother Righteous demands it."

The faeries leapt into the air agitated. "Gives us worth." "We must serve her."

Aura held up her hand to quiet their chatter. "Layla is wrong."

The other faeries gasped at Aura's boldness.

Aura continued. "Faeries press emotions. This is what keeps us alive in Velona."

Abbie rocked in her chair, giving Karole room to make her observations and to process what the faeries were saying. Karole glanced at Abbie then turned back to the faeries. "What do you mean? It is your worth?"

The faeries all landed delicately on the desk. Aura stood closest to Abbie. Diamond animatedly spoke to Aura. Aura shrugged one shoulder, her wings snapped taut behind her, and then folded against her back. "She… She doesn't allow…"

Diamond turned to Abbie. "Mother Righteous banned love a long, long, long, long, long—"

Aura pushed Diamond down. She rolled back on her bottom. Aura finished, "Time ago."

She paced back and forth, while Diamond slowly recovered her stance. She glared at Aura. Abbie couldn't be sure, she had given the magnifying glass to her sister, but she swore Diamond stuck out her tongue at Aura and blew a raspberry.

Abbie snorted a chuckle. Obviously this mother righteous had a tyrannical reign over these faeries and it was a subject that caused them a great deal of anxiety.

Another faerie approached the front of the standing swarm. "Love has been forgotten by most." Another came forward. "But some still believe…" Then another. "that it exists." Aura shoved them back and took the dominate position.

All of the faeries finished in unison, "But we *saw* it."

Diamond stepped forward. "With you and… him."

Aura hung her head. "I'm sorry we pushed anger on him."

Amethyst nodded. "Our normal way is the normal way. But we can stop, here."

Diamond stepped out of the cluster. "Mother Righteous's power is not felt… here."

Another faerie spoke up. "In Velona, when we see *good* feelings, we squash it." She slammed her fist into her palm.

Aura darted a quick glance toward her and back to Abbie. "You understand?"

Abbie swallowed. "I suppose I do understand about normal ways, but I don't understand why anyone would want a world where love didn't exist."

Aura shrugged. "It is Mother Righteous's normal way." Another faerie flew up just hovering above the desk top. "She rules Velona." Yet another swooped next to the second. "She is the Queen."

Aura glared at her sisters. "Amethyst, Diamond! I can tell her." She turned back to Abbie. "We think love hurt our Queen long ago. She demanded love be… removed… for so long." Another faerie flew out. "We thought it was this way everywhere." She nodded reassuringly.

Aura fluttered as if to block her. "Not all of us thought it a myth. I knew." Aura drew in a deep breath and let it out slowly. "I hoped. But I know now."

Abbie frowned. "Yeah, about that. You know, I just met Dr. Assad." She glanced at Karole. "I mean, I've wanted to meet him before. He's attractive, but—"

"Oh. There's so much more!" Aura seemed to puff out her chest. "Your prism stream aligned. It was beautiful. It was small, thin, but my guess is it will only grow stronger."

Abbie squinted. "Grow… stronger? How could you possibly—"

"Wait a minute." Karole leaned closer to Aura. "If this mother righteous has banned love, how do you know that's what you saw?"

Aura hovered in front of Karole's face. The faerie looked thoughtful. "We… just… know."

Karole drew back. "Hmm. Interesting."

Abbie gasped. "Oh good grief, what time is it?"

Karole turned her watch on her wrist and checked the time. "Six o'clock."

"We're supposed to meet Joseph at The Oasis." She turned to the faeries. "How on earth am I going to go with these… faeries hanging all over me?"

"Maybe we can put them in a box or something."

The faeries took flight and vanished into Abbie's hair.

Abbie stared at her sister. "Something tells me that won't work."

Karole smirked a mischievous smile. "Gee, why?"

A tickling sensation crawled across Abbie's head and traversed down her neck. She shivered.

"Well." Karole lifted her brow. "We missed the debriefing. I don't have any idea what they are telling everybody, but my guess is they are denying everything. They may even be requiring all witnesses to the… accident to stay on-site."

Abbie shrugged. "But The Oasis is on-site."

"Well, if you want to have this first date with Joseph, I suggest you make… your little friends understand that they've gotta stay here, or something."

Abbie rotated her eyeball to the farthest most corner of her socket in an attempt to see even one faerie. "You hear that? If I walk out of this office, you've *got* to stay here."

"We stay with you!" All the little voices squeaked from under her hair.

She looked into her sister's face, and smiled as if Karole were taking her picture. "How do I look?"

"Disheveled."

"Ugh. I've got a shower here in my lab and a change of clothes, but how can I get cleaned up with faeries in my hair?" Abbie dropped her head into her hands. "Who am I kidding? I can't go to The Oasis with faeries in my hair! Somebody will see them and then they'll know they came from that fog, and then all hell will break loose."

Karole's eyes roved over Abbie's head and the faeries protruding between the strands. "Can they get out of your hair long enough for you to take a shower?"

Tears sprang to Abbie's eyes "I have no idea."

Chapter Eight

Karole drove her red Dodge Charger the half mile around the VEIL facility's paved road from her sister's QuESO Department to The Oasis Cantina near the east gate. She had no idea if Joseph Assad would be there or if *anybody* would be there, but she'd promised her sister she'd try.

She pulled into The Oasis's parking lot astounded by the number of vehicles. "Will you look at this…" she said to herself.

So many cars and trucks. It was the fullest she'd ever seen this lot, any lot, for that matter, at VEIL. She supposed nearly *everybody* was here. And why not? Those who experienced the accident would naturally end up here. Alcohol and camaraderie. People needed to wind down with a drink and talk about what happened.

Karole drove slowly, but there were no empty spaces. Finally, she parked in front of the end vehicle parallel parked along the road leading to the east gate. This would be a bit of a hike, but she'd promised Abbie.

People inside The Oasis were four to a two top, six and eight to a four top. They stood between the stools where others sat at the bar. They leaned against the outer walls. A large group of scientists were frantically filling up napkins with scribbles. Probably trying to figure out what went wrong. Better to write on the napkins then to start writing on the walls, Karole mused. Not that it couldn't happen. This bar was on-site for a reason and anyone who worked here was fully cleared for Top Secret exposure. They did that for the brainiacs to be able to talk through their obscure calculations over a beer or coffee without exposing secrets to the non-cleared civilian population in Loville.

She walked into the bar, leaned past Sandy East, who slumped over a glass of wine, and signaled to the bartender she wanted a drink. Sandy smiled but it didn't look joyful. Karole smiled back with a practiced *everything's-going-to-be-alright* smile that doctors just naturally learn to give people.

Bert, the bartender, approached Karole with a peaked eyebrow. His way of asking what she wanted. "I'll have a Pepsi and lime."

His response consisted of his head tipping back. He went about making her drink. She tossed a five-dollar bill on the bar and he gave her change. Sandy's eyes leveled with Karole's.

"I heard the whole facility went on lock down. Has it

been lifted yet?"

Sandy nodded. "Yeah. Stettler told everybody it was a small accident, but everything was being taken care of." She gulped her wine. "He told everyone to take the day off, and tomorrow, let's resume work like normal. Except the Ops Center staff. We said we could take a few days off, with pay, but we must remember anything that happens out here is top secret." A laugh seemed forced, then caught in her throat, like a hiccup. "That's why everybody's here. Nobody *wants* to go home. It was just too… weird."

Karole touched Sandy's shoulder. "It only makes sense everybody would end up here at The Oasis. This is where we *can* talk about it."

Sandy nodded and lifted two fingers toward the bartender. Bert refilled her glass. "Yeah. I guess you're right. From the looks on these faces, there's more processing than talking going on. But I get what you're saying. This *is* the only bar with clearance for top secret conversations."

Karole nodded.

Sandy tipped her head toward the table of scientists. "See, they end up here trying to figure out what went wrong with that experiment. I wonder why Holly Teak isn't here? There's her lab-buddy."

Karole let her eyes rove over the others sitting along the walls, then she perused the tables. She knew nearly everyone in this bar.

She spotted Assad sitting alone in a two-top booth. "Um, excuse me, Sandy. There's someone here I need to speak to."

Sandy looked over her wine glass at Karole as she swigged the last dregs. "Oh, sure." She wiped spilled wine from her lip and held up two fingers for Bert.

Karole hesitated before leaving. "You know, you should consider staying in a temporary apartment tonight. It's what they are here for."

She waited until Sandy nodded.

"That's what Stettler said, too." Her speech was slurred. Karole hoped she took him up on the offer.

She pushed her way through standing people to get to the booth where Assad sat. "Mind if I sit down?"

He looked up with a smile and instantly frowned. "I thought you were Abbie. I never realized how much you two sound alike."

Karole sat. "Yeah, we've been told that most of our lives. I think she sounds more like Mother. I guess that means I sound like Mother…"

He smiled with a slight chuckle. Karole took her time, diagnosing what his morose appearance meant. Did he want to see Abbie tonight, even after the… incident with the faeries on the mountain? She assessed he probably did. "So. You are here because there's nowhere else to go that's safe to talk about what happened, or… are you really waiting to see my sister?"

His eyes popped up to her. "Honestly, I had hoped to see Abbie. Then I thought we'd—" Concern washed over his face. "Is she alright? Those things didn't hurt her, did they?"

"No!" Karole held up her hand to stop him from speaking. "Shh. Don't say anything specific. She wants to see you too. It's just that… she, we felt it was best for her to stay in her office. I, she wanted me to see if you wanted to go there… where it's more private."

He stared at her as if he were deciphering what she wasn't saying. "She's alright?"

"Yes."

"Then, sure. I'll go to her office." He slid out of the booth and extended a hand to Karole. She smiled and slid out on her own. "You're very sweet. I see why she likes you."

"She does?" Joseph paused.

"Well, sure. You think I'd come here if she didn't really want to see you?"

"Oh. Right." He took Karole's elbow and guided her through the crowd.

"Okay, my little friends. I need to take a shower and you need to give me some space." Abbie waited. She could feel the faeries squirming around on her scalp. "Please let me wash my hair."

She jerked the shower curtain back. "See, this is a shower. I'm going to take off all my clothes and get in. You can—"

She looked around the small bathroom. "You can sit here on the curtain rod and watch."

She cringed. Having over a dozen little creatures watching her take a shower felt… weird. But it was better than trying to wash her hair with them in it. She patted the top of the rod. Aura flew out, then another followed. Soon all the faeries sat in a line on the rod, like small birds on the phone lines. Abbie giggled. "You remind me of my sister's sun visor when Sonic had those collectible plastic animals on their straws."

They seated themselves with their legs crossed at the ankles and waited, like a chorus line of Rockettes. "Good. Now—"

She disrobed and climbed in the shower, letting the water run until it was warm enough then pulled the lever that made the shower head spray. The faeries wiggled with excitement. "It's like the waterfall in Velona." Aura flew out to inspect the water flow.

Abbie backed into the stream and applied shampoo.

"Oooo." Aura dashed toward Abbie's hair. The others followed. "We like these, white things. What are they called?"

Abbie shook her head. "I thought you agreed to stay on the curtain rod."

"Bubbles are fun!" Diamond giggled as she dove under the frothy foam.

Abbie considered how Diamond had found the answer to her question. They must be able to hear Abbie's thoughts. Obviously. When she first encountered them, they did speak directly into her mind.

Aura flopped onto her back as if swimming across the shampoo using the back stroke. Amethyst cackled a laugh that made Abbie laugh too. "Yes. I suppose they are. But I need you to go back to the rod. I have to scrub my head, and I'm afraid I'll hurt you."

Abbie acknowledged another oddity. She knew what they were doing even though she couldn't see them. It was as if their minds remained connected… like the beehive she had compared them to earlier.

The faeries reluctantly returned to the rod. Tiny bubbles clung to their crystal shards of hair and wings.

"We like shampoo!" Aura squeaked. Diamond's legs swung from the curtain rod. "Fun, fun, fun!"

Another faerie almost fell from the rod, giggling. Her wings dashed out to save her balance. "Bubbles fun!"

Abbie laughed with them as she finished her shower. With her hair dried and her clothes changed, she sat down at her desk. The faeries landed on the blotter. They sparkled after the bath. Abbie smiled, then turned her attention to the door and sighed.

Would Karole find Joseph? Would he agree to come to her office? Abbie chewed her lip as she waited. A knock with a series of raps startled the faeries and they all zipped into her hair to hide. The pattern of the knocking told Abbie it was her sister at the door. She always knocked to the rhythm of *Shave and a Haircut, Two Bits*. "It's alright. It's just Karole."

She called out, "Come in!"

Karole opened the door and stood back, letting Joseph enter first.

"Joseph!" Abbie leapt to her feet. Faeries lagged behind her swift movement, they caught up with her and dove into her hair.

Joseph's eyes went wide. "I see those things are still… with you."

"Yes." Abbie turned slightly away from him. She had showered and changed clothes, hoping she looked less disheveled. "I convinced them to give me a little space so I could clean up. It worked for the most part."

"For the most part? What do you mean?" Joseph jerked his gaze to Karole as she walked past him to sit on a stool. He seemed to have been startled by her. Had he forgotten she was still there? Abbie smiled. "Well, actually it's kind of a funny story."

He smiled but worry lingered in his eyes. "Are you alright?"

"Oh. Yes. We're fine." She almost patted her hair but remembered the faeries were there and awkwardly put her hand down. "They are just scared for the most part and feel safer when they are… on me."

He nodded, examining her hair.

Aura rose up above Abbie's curls, with a handful of strands in each hand— what was she doing, braiding Abbie's hair?—and Aura smiled sheepishly. Joseph exhaled a chuckle. Aura dove back down.

Abbie shivered. "Burururur. They tickle." She giggled.

"Are you sure they are… safe?" He continued to look at her hair as if he were observing maggots.

"Joseph. Yes. They don't want to hurt me… or you."

His eyes darted to hers. "Then how do you expl— I don't know what happened out there?" His face reddened as if he were getting angry. "I felt my temper twist into something beyond my control! I think they had something to do with… manipulating my mind."

Abbie turned her thoughts to the Faeries. *Are you doing this?*

"Not us." Aura responded in Abbie's mind. *"But he*

doesn't trust us."

"Well! Can you blame him?" Abbie lifted her gaze to Joseph. "Back outside of Lab One, where we saw the faeries come out of the fog, they had just crossed over… from their world." She paused to see if he followed.

His eyes hardened, but he didn't say anything.

She continued. "They *did* manipulate your emotions."

"See! I knew it. We need to do something… to protect ourselves. You shouldn't have them swarming your head like that—"

Abbie chuckled. "What do you want us to do, put aluminum foil on our heads?"

He stiffened. "You're laughing at my mind being manipulated by an alien. Look—" He turned to Karole. "I don't care how cute *you* may think they are. They're dangerous!" He jerked back to face Abbie. "¿Comprendo?"

Abbie stepped up to him, gently taking his hands into hers. "Joseph. I know they are… different. But it's not like they're from Jupiter and invading our planet. Please listen to me."

Aura and Diamond lifted out of Abbie's hair. "We sorry." "We not know." "Making mad is our normal." "Abbie told us we do not have to." "Please, for-give."

Joseph jerked back from her touch, staring at the two faeries, his jaw slack. "If I didn't know better, I'd think they were honestly sincere in their apology."

"They are sincere." Abbie stepped closer.

"But— how do I know that? How do I know they are not… *influencing* my mind to believe I can trust them?"

Abbie took a step back from Joseph. "Joseph, I'm trying to say we caused this. They are here because of what we did in that Lab One experiment." She considered his anxious expression. "How about this— Girls! Front and center."

Every faerie flew out and above her head then swooped down to hover between her and Joseph. "Girls, explain to Joseph why he can trust you."

Aura began, "We love love."

The others continued. "You have love." "Mother Righteous not here." "She make us squash love." The littlest faerie smashed her tiny fist into her hand.

"We want to … study love." Aura finished.

"Love?" Joseph turned his gaze to Karole, then Abbie. "But, we aren't—"

Abbie smiled. "I know, of course not, but my conclusions are that whoever this mother righteous is has set a precedent for the faeries to use their… talents… to suppress happy emotions. Now that they have escaped to our world, they have come to their own conclusions that they are no longer bound by her demands. They did what they did to you because they didn't yet know it was okay not to. I believe we can trust them, because they are just as fascinated with our emotions as we are with their existence."

Joseph rubbed the back of his neck. "This is not quantifiable." He collapsed in an office chair. "I just don't think I— what is this *other world* you keep speaking of. How is that even possible?"

Abbie shrugged. "You know the projected effects of quantum entanglement better than I. It seems you and Doctor Teak accomplished something far beyond your expectations. You, somehow, entangled two dimensions. And I think that quartz wall in the mountain just outside Lab One is the portal." She squeezed her eyes closed. "That, or it's the fog, I haven't really figured it all out yet. I need to get back in there and examine that quartz."

Karole leapt to her feet. "You can't."

Abbie turned to look at her. "What? Why?"

"She's right." Joseph nodded. "At the facility-wide meeting Stettler told everyone he's shut down operations in Quantum Lab One until further notice."

"He can't do that!" Abbie swirled to glare at Joseph. "Can he? How are we going to figure out what happened? How is Holly—"

Her eyes darted around the swarm of faeries flying above her head. "Is Holly alright?"

"I don't know." Joseph shrugged. "I haven't seen her or Axel since... you know."

Abbie followed the switch back flights of the faeries.

"We can't let anybody know about these… faeries."

Joseph stood. "No! Proper protocol states that unknown findings must be reported within twenty-four hours of discovery."

"Well, that's tomorrow. For now, I don't want to tell anybody about them, until I have a better understanding of who they are and where they came from… and how we caused this to happen."

The faeries blinked as one, as if cued by some connected mental thought.

A slight grin lifted on one side of Joseph's mouth. "They seem to be connected in thought, a lot like our entangled photons. When one moves, the other moves. Interesting." He floated his eyes over each faerie, taking in the similarities and differences among them. "They really are fascinating."

"Ah!" He jumped back. "How do I know if that's my own thought or them projecting that idea into my head?"

Abbie's eyes widened. "I don't know. You just… have to… believe."

Should she tell him the story of Tinker Bell and how Peter Pan had to believe in order for the little faerie to recover from the poisoning?

"One thing I do know." Joseph shook his head, as if to clear faerie dust from his mind. "I might agree with you to keep this quiet for now. It's not standard operating procedure, but— and I don't think you should leave the facility. I assume you live in town, not in the temporary apartments, like Doctor Teak?"

"Right." Abbie nodded. "I have a rental in Loville. Karole does too." Abbie tilted her head, processing what he had said. "Holly still lives in the temporary apartments?"

Joseph looked at Karole then Abbie. "Yeah, she's been so focused on making all this happen that she never took the time to find a place in town." He shrugged.

Abbie slowly moved her head, absorbing this insightful information about the intense scientist. "That actually explains a lot."

Joseph continued. "Well, I heard Stettler was letting anyone who wanted to stay on-site take a temporary apartment. It's just a matter of requesting one. No questions asked." He looked at Karole as if he were checking for concurrence.

Karole nodded slowly. "That's probably a good idea, Abbie. That way you minimize the probability of exposing these little creatures to real people. "

"They're not creatures!" Abbie turned angry eyes on her sister. "They are faeries!"

"Okay!" Karole held up a hand of surrender. "Now, how do we get you out of here and across the facility to the apartments without *them* being seen?"

Abbie snapped her fingers. "I have a hoodie. If they

hide in my hair and I put the hood up… maybe."

"I guess it's all we've got. You have to look as natural as possible. Not like we can throw a blanket over your head and try to pull that off as nothing-is-wrong." Karole tapped her chin. Her thinking pose. "I can go to your house and get your things, say… enough for a week?"

She glanced at Joseph. He nodded. "And I'll go get you some groceries."

"What!" Abbie jerked back to him. "No. You don't need—"

"I want to." Joseph smiled, then frowned. He glared at the faeries. "At least I think I want to."

Chapter Nine

Joseph helped Abbie slip into the grey hoodie. He leaned away from the swarming creatures. Constantly analyzing his own feelings to monitor if he thought they were affecting his thinking. Gingerly he lifted the hood and Abbie took hold of the top edge, easing it over the parasitic addition to Abbie's hair. She turned to him. "How do I look?"

He feigned approval. "Like you have your hair in some kind of body-building curlers."

Abbie chuckled. "What do you know about body-building curlers?"

He shrugged. "Seven sisters, remember?"

"Ah." She tipped her head back.

Karole lead the way. Joseph took Abbie's elbow. Abbie tucked a laptop computer under her arm. Joseph lifted his cell phone to call security. "Yes, this is Doctor Assad, Dr. Abbie Crossan would like to accept a temporary apartment for tonight. I will be escorting her to the buildings. Can someone meet us there to give her a key?"

He nodded. "Good. We'll be there in a few minutes."

They walked to the parking lot between their two buildings. Joseph put Abbie in the passenger side of Karole's car.

"Give me your locker key, I'll go get your cell phone." He trotted off to his car.

The guard handed Joseph the cell phone without question. "Thank you. With all the excitement, she forgot all about this." He tossed the phone in the air and caught it.

Rushing back to his Jag, he caught up with Karole who drove just under the speed limit around to the other side where the apartments stood. "Good. Don't call any attention to yourselves," he muttered as if they could hear him.

His eyes remained on the grey hoodie on the right. He really liked this woman. She was smart. The equation she had written on Teak's white board was very impressive. She obviously had a level of understanding about quantum physics that he wouldn't expect from a geologist. She had a unique perspective on life. Who would dye their hair pink otherwise?

He'd spied her in the cafeteria over the last few weeks. Everyday at lunch, precisely at eleven-fifty, she and her sister entered. He had made sure to arrive at eleven-forty, so he could watch for an opportunity to introduce himself. Then it was the bold sister who pranced across the eatery to make sure Abbie was introduced to him. He chuckled at the memory.

Was that just today? So much had happened since that quiet but engaging encounter. He still had the "prescription" in his pocket with Abbie's phone number. Karole had written, "Please call her," and scrawled the number. Just like a medical doctor's illegible script. He had intended to meet her for a drink at The Oasis, as her sister had said, then if that went well, he had hoped to ask her to go out to dinner. Take it slow and easy. Get to know her, she get to know him.

Then the accident. Out of sheer instinct he found himself covering her body with his. The adrenaline rush and the warmth of her body under him left a brand on his heart. His emotions were accelerated and he now found himself longing to be with her. To see that she was alright, safe. Then those… creatures—

Now he wasn't sure if what he felt was real. What strange little aliens they were. Some sort of telepathic enhanced hive mentality in such a small brained animal.

He stiffened. Were they animal? Or humanoid? How could he shield his mind from their influence?

He pulled into the parking area behind the temporary apartments and rushed over to open Abbie's door. She eased out of the car while he held her elbow. A flood of emotions swamped his heart. He wanted to take her into his arms and tell her everything would be alright. He would protect her.

She smiled wryly. He leaned toward her intending to tenderly kiss those uncertain lips.

Wait! Joseph jumped back

Is this the faeries' doing, again? He looked closely under her hoodie. There was slight movement. "They have got to be absolutely still for this to work," he whispered.

Abbie nodded. The movements slowed down and stopped. Had she spoken to them in her mind? The way they had spoken to both her and him when they first came out of the fog? He had heard them in his native language. It was mind-blowing!

With her hood not looking like a sack filled with mice, he walked her to the entry door of one of the apartment buildings. The guard had said to come to the south building. Joseph exhaled and opened the door for Abbie.

She walked in ahead of him and smiled at Frank. "Oh. Frank. Thank you."

"My pleasure, Dr. Abbie." He stood next to a metal box on the wall and handed her a card key, like a motel. He looked tired. This was probably going on thirteen hours for his normally eight-hour shift. "3-G, stairs are there"—he pointed like the airline steward— "elevator is across the hall, third floor, and down the hall about halfway. Let us know if you need anything. The apartments should be fully equipped with everything you need, except food and your clothes, of course."

"Right. Thank you." She took the key and turned to Joseph. "Stairs or elevator?"

"Let's take the stairs." Joseph took her elbow again, casually blocking Frank's view of Abbie just in case the parasites decided to wriggle around, and walked her across the hall.

Abbie nodded and tucked the key in her pants pocket. They climbed the stairs in that same cadence, like when they had entered Lab One's Observation Area before. Karole followed silently behind. Abbie lead the way down the hall. She unlocked the door and walked in, Joseph and Karole with her. Abbie let out a huge sigh.

"That went well." Joseph understood her relief.

She looked around the apartment. "So. This is home away from home."

"Sí. I lived here for a week, when I first came onboard. Once I found an apartment in town, I moved. Most everyone did. Except Dr. Teak." Joseph chuckled.

"Yeah, you mentioned that earlier." Abbie pushed the hood off her head.

Joseph walked into the kitchen, opening cabinets. "I figured it would be better than you trying to sleep on a cot in your office." He let his eyes rove over the Ikea furniture. "I suppose I was right."

Abbie walked into his arms, he automatically wrapped them around her, hoping she couldn't hear his heart speed up.

"Thank you." Her voice was muffled against his chest.

"You're welcome." He rubbed her back and pulled her away from him. "Now, I'll be back in thirty minutes, forty at most. What do you want to eat?"

Sadness filled her eyes. "I don't care, really. Whatever you choose is fine with me." She glanced at the little kitchen.

"There're pots and pans." Karole spoke for the first time. Joseph and Abbie jerked. Had she forgotten her sister was there too? He certainly had.

"This looks fine." Joseph examined her hair. The creatures emerged and flew above her head. They seemed to be looking around at the new location. "I'll be back as soon as I can. Are you sure you're alright? With them… alone?"

"Of course." She forced a chuckle. "Don't go to a lot of trouble. A TV dinner will be fine, just… remember to get something sweet for the faeries." Abbie sounded sad, he almost suggested they order pizza instead. But he'd still have to leave her to go pick it up at the gate. A home cooked Lebanese meal would be better. He shook his head. "I have something much better in mind, and I'll get the… them something tasty from the bakery. I won't be long." He kissed her forehead. It felt so natural to kiss her before he walked away. This had been a strange day. And he could only imagine it getting stranger.

She pursed her lips and nodded slightly.

Joseph tore himself from her brave façade and walked toward the door.

"Wait." Karole said. "I'll go with you." She turned to Abbie and briefly discussed what all she needed from her home, then hurried to join Joseph. She spoke over her shoulder to Abbie. "Try to relax while we are gone, Doctor's orders."

Abbie smiled and closed the door.

Once he was in the hall, he felt much less reluctant to leave her. It was the right thing to do, to get her some groceries, since she couldn't leave the facility. Of course Karole could have bought food, but Karole couldn't possibly know the right ingredients for what he had in mind. Besides, he really didn't mind doing it, as a favor for a friend.

Was that what Abbie was now? A friend? A friend that he felt compelled to kiss before he walked away from? He stopped midstride. When he was near her… and the faeries, he had much stronger feelings for her. He would make sure he kept that in check when he came back. This wasn't like him— to leap into a relationship like he seemed to be doing with Abbie.

Granted, she was different, he could admit to that. But…

"Are you okay?" Karole's voice startled him out of his

thoughts. Once again, he had forgotten she was there. "Yes. It's just… hard to…"

"Process?" Karole offered.

"Yes."

She nodded. "Believe me, I know."

Joseph pushed the elevator button. He needed to keep his emotions in check until he knew for sure the source of his feelings. Abbie's sister was nothing more than an acquaintance to him, he didn't know her well enough to divulge his concerns. But something told him he would be getting to know her quite well over the next few…

"Stop!" Joseph blurted to no one.

Karole jumped.

Joseph shook his head. "I'm sorry. I've got a lot going on in my head."

Karole smiled. "That's understandable."

The elevator doors opened. Frank was gone. The hall looked empty. Joseph gestured for Karole to exit first, he followed behind her. "See you in a little while."

"Yeah, see ya."

Abbie's strength drained from her limbs. Complete exhaustion pulled her down onto the modular sofa. Maybe she should have let Karole examine her. Aura flew out into her visual range, hovering in front of her face. "We are alright."

"I know you are." She considered her own words. She did know. How did she know? "It's me I'm concerned about."

Aura swooped around as if looking Abbie over. "You are not… injured?"

"No, I'm not injured. I'm just… drained."

Diamond flew out, hovering next to Aura. "What is drained? Are you hungry? Do you need some crystalized honey?" Diamond rubbed her abdomen. "I'm thinking I need some. Do you have any?"

Abbie sighed heavily. "I don't think so." She forced herself to stand and drudged to the efficient little kitchen. She opened cabinet doors and drawers. "We have everything we need to live here…"

The faeries fluttered in the air with excitement.

"…except food."

Fluttering dissolved into disappointed shrugs. They folded their wings and landed delicately on the little bar jutting out between the kitchen and the sitting room. Two stools sat on the opposite side of the bar, making a reasonable place to sit and eat. Abbie leaned a hip on one stool, then scooted onto the center. With a sigh, she placed her chin in her palm. "Joseph is buying groceries. I asked him to remember you. Maybe he'll think to bring some honey too."

"Can we ask him?"

"Well, I— don't have his number. Wait, maybe I do." Abbie lifted her phone, scanned through some apps, and finally opened the VEIL on-site phone directory. It was classified, of course, but she had access. She scrolled through to find Joseph. "Ah. Here it is." She touched the hyperlink and waited for him to answer. Suddenly, she reconsidered openly speaking about the faeries. This event had been classified Extra Sensitive Top Secret far as she knew.

"Hello?" Joseph answered. Tranquil jazz music played behind his voice. He must be at the grocery store.

"Joseph, It's me… Abbie."

He chuckled. "Yes? Are you alright?"

"I'm fine. I have a request. You know, I have over a dozen sweet tooths here and they seem to think only crystalized honey will do."

She cringed. Hopefully he understood what she was getting at and didn't think she had lost her mind.

"Ah. Fresh honey crystalizes, I believe. I'll see what I can find."

"Sounds good. Thank you."

"You're welcome, I'm almost done here. I should be back in less than twenty minutes."

"Good. We are hungry." She started, regretting having said *we*. "I-I mean, aren't you hungry too?"

He chuckled, "Yes, as a matter of fact I am, so you're right, *we* are hungry."

Good. He understood and didn't give the secret away. "Thank you. We- I'll be waiting."

"Okay. *Adiós*."

She disconnected, then jerked her phone up. She'd forgotten to say bye! What was wrong with her? She'd never hung up on someone without saying goodbye. She looked at the faeries. They seemed happy that Joseph would bring sweets for them. A feeling of elation washed over her, too. Maybe he'd bring her a cream-cheese cake with nuts…

That was odd, she hardly ever craved cake. What was he planning for supper? What about breakfast? Would he think to buy cereal? Milk? Why hadn't she made a list? How could she expect a perfect stranger to know what she'd want to stock her kitchen?

Take what you get and don't throw a fit. She heard the childhood mantra she had been told so many times. That was right. She needed to be grateful for whatever Joseph bought. Besides, she could always send Karole to get anything else she needed. Karole knew her brand of cereal and TV dinners.

A high-pitched chanting caught her attention, bringing her out of her self-absorbed thought. "Take what you get…

don't throw a fit."

The faeries were saying the line, like a cheerleading squad, separated into two sides. Half said the "Take what you get," and the other side threw it back at them, "don't throw a fit."

A smile sprang to Abbie's lips. How cute! Then the reality of their chanting struck her hard. She had not said it out loud. They talked to her in her head. It was becoming more and more obvious they listened, too. A creepy shiver rolled over her spine. This was going to take some getting used to.

A knock on the door. Abbie jerked to her feet with a gasp. Her hand shot up to her chest. *Calm down. It's gotta be Karole... or Joseph.* Shaking her head at how foolish she was being, she crossed the room and opened the door.

Karole swept in with a suitcase, duffle bag, and a really large purse that Abbie had never seen before. "Wow. Thanks. What's in the carryon?"

Karole feigned embarrassment. "You didn't have anything big enough for your toiletries, so I stopped at the Dollar Store and bought you a beach bag purse."

"Ah." Abbie was impressed. Her sister wasn't usually this thoughtful. "Well, thank you. Here let me take those." She reached for the duffle and big bag. "I'll put these away."

"Okay, and I'll hang up your clothes." Karole took the suitcase into the bedroom. Abbie heard drawers open and close. She was putting her foldables away too. Abbie sighed. Would she be stuck here that long?

Abbie distributed her toiletries in the bathroom cabinet, hung up towels, and lined up her vitamins on the counter. She put shower stuff behind the white plastic curtain and turned to find the faeries inspecting everything. "We can play in your bubbles?"

Abbie sighed. This was her life now. Taking a shower with faeries playing in the bubbles she made. How long would she be dealing with these faeries? The rest of her life? A bolt of dread pierced her gut. She had loved the idea of Tinker Bell all of her life, but the reality of a flock of faeries actually living with her, and being so… attached to her was a whole other matter. One that she tired of already.

Just as that thought passed through her mind, she felt a sensation of warmth and companionship wash over her. The faeries were comforting. Knowing they were always there with her. She would never be alone, ever. Joy filled her heart. Safety in numbers. Security with the swarm.

She watched as Aura and Diamond discuss a container of body wash. "Oranges." "Hmmm, it smells sweet." "Look at this" Diamond flew to the shampoo bottle. "Mixed berries? Remember?" "Yes. It smells like Abbie." Just then a scream caused all the faeries to turn toward the built-in shelf.

"I'm stuck! I'm stuck! I'm stuck! It's eating me! I'm

going to die!" Amethyst was caught in the shower scrubby. Abbie tsked her tongue and reached over to gently ease her out of the gathered netting. "You have to be careful. Curiosity killed the cat, you know."

Amethyst's eyes were larger than usual. "Cat? There's a cat here, too?"

"No, silly. It's just an expression."

Karole stopped at the bathroom door. "Okay, I'm all done. How's it going in— what happened?"

"Oh Amethyst got caught in the scrubber and panicked."

Karole tipped her head back. "I see. Well, let's all be careful with the things that we are not familiar with." She glared at Abbie.

Another knock on the door drew their attention, and Abbie rushed to answer it. This time it *had* to be Joseph. A sense of bliss filled her heart. She almost skipped to the door. Breathless, she pulled the knob. "Hi." She panted.

He looked at her oddly, recyclable bags hung from his arms. But his hands were encumbered with a large box.

"Goodness! Did you leave anything in the store?" Abbie giggled.

Joseph peeked around the box. "I got something that I hope will help."

He approached the bar and leaned to one side, verifying it was clear, then put the box down. He moved to the counter, looked at the surface, and removed the bags from his arms.

Abbie smiled. How thoughtful of him to first check that no faeries were on the bar or counter. A sigh came out of nowhere and escaped her lips. She resisted grasping her hands together and holding them next to her cheek. In her peripheral, she noticed the faeries, collectively doing that very thing.

She cleared her throat and rushed to help put things away. "So, what's in the box?"

He smiled. "I went by that Mystique Emporium. Blaze Moonstar had this in her window. She was closed, of course, but I know she stays in the apartment above the store sometimes, so I went around back and got her to open the store. I think it was part of her window dressing, but I told her it was an emergency."

He opened the folded flaps and lifted onto his tiptoes to get a grip on the thing inside. He pulled it upward. A dark blue wooden structure emerged. Abbie watched intently until she realized what he had bought.

"A doll house!" Abbie clasped her hands. "How'd you convince Blaze a doll house was an emergency?"

"I told her my niece was in town and it was her birthday." He grinned and waggled his eyebrows.

"Clever!" Abbie turned to the faeries. "Look! Aura, Diamond, Amethyst! Joseph bought you a house."

The faeries swarmed the little structure. Open on one side, the other looked like a white two-story colonial house with a red door and a dark-blue roof. Joseph turned it around so the faeries could see both floors at once. They fussed and squeaked as they walked through it. Sitting on the miniature furniture and laying on the beds. Aura flew out.

"It's wonderful!" She wiped a crystal tear and tossed it aside. "We are so happy!"

"Good." Joseph turned away and removed food from the grocery sacks. "My thought is, if they like the doll house, perhaps we can convince them to stay in it, and you can go back to work… without them." He looked at Abbie, worry filled his eyes.

"Seems like a good idea to me." Abbie smiled as she rushed to help him. "Ground lamb? Bread crumbs, mangos… what are you making?"

He set jars of different flavored honeys on the bar beside the bags, a box of individually wrapped pound cakes, a container of vanilla icing, and a glass spice jar labeled saffron. Abbie tilted her head to inspect the contents. It looked like tiny branches of coral.

"Gosh. You didn't have to buy so much! But thank you."

"It is my pleasure." He separated some of the groceries, placing them next to the two-burner stove. The rest he handed to her to put away.

"You two work like you've done this together a long time." Karole stood in the sitting room as if in awe, staring at Abbie and Joseph.

Heat rose on Abbie's neck and fill her cheeks. "Just putting away groceries, Karole. Don't make a *big deal* about it."

Karole shrugged. "I'll be going. Call me if you need anything else. And don't worry. Surely this will all be straightened out soon."

"Worried. Why would I be worried?" Abbie furrowed her brow.

Karole's face morphed into that look Abbie had seen before. That this-is-not-good look she gets just before she tells someone really bad news.

Abbie stared at her sister. "What?"

"Nothing. I'll call you in the morning." Karole turned to the vibrating doll house. "Good night girls! I like your little house."

A buzz of excitement replied. Karole smiled at Abbie, then Joseph. "This was a good idea, Assad."

Joseph tossed his head back with a smile and continued with making supper.

Abbie walked her sister to the door. "Okay. Good night." She watched Karole walk down the hall.

She turned back to the apartment. Joseph stood gaping at her. "What?"

Joseph drew in a deep breath. "Come sit down, Abbie. I'll make dinner and—"

Abbie followed his line of sight. The faeries were ripping open the box of cakes, biting through the plastic. Joseph stepped over and tore open a package. They dove into the opening and pulled handfuls out, stuffing it into their mouths. Three others were pounding on the plastic lid to the icing. He opened it and pealed back the foil. They scooped handfuls of icing and crammed it into their mouths. Still others fluttered with excitement over the honeys trying to get them open. He turned to the counter and twisted off the lids. They dove over the edge and drew the honey into their mouths like a horse at a pond.

"I think they were hungry," Abbie mused, her words slurred slightly. Joseph turned a curious gaze to her. "Are you alright?"

"Shhure. Why?"

Joseph considered her a moment. "You almost sound drunk." He examined her eyes, pulled down her bottom eye lid.

The faeries, flew into the air, disoriented, crashing into each other, roiling in the air like boiling water and scattered into Abbie's hair. She winced. The faeries tangled and stuck to her hair from the honey and icing on their hands. She staggered. Joseph grabbed her shoulders. "You better sit down." He eased her onto the sofa.

"Let me get some food in you." He rushed to the kitchenette and tore off a piece of flat-bread and smeared something on it. "Here, eat this while I get things ready."

"Hmm. Garlic. I love garlic butter." Abbie purred as she nibbled the hunk of bread. "You got any sugar I can put on this."

Joseph looked up from mixing ground lamb in a bowl. "Do you customarily eat sugar with garlic bread?"

"No. But I was just thinking it would taste really good together."

Joseph stared at her. "Okay." He grabbed a dish towel and washed his hand in the sink. "Listen to me. Normally, *no one* wants sugar with garlic. I think the faeries… have an influence over you."

"Um, Aura. I need you and your… sisters to get in your little house." He watched while they came out of Abbie's hair and fluttered erratically to the doll house. Abbie smiled. His eyes roved over the faeries in the house. They laid on various pieces of furniture, one was even in the little bathtub. Anywhere they could lay down, they settled and instantly were asleep.

Abbie blinked slowly and then felt something like a fog lifting from her mind. She sat up straighter. "I- I've been wondering the same thing." She spoke quietly, not to disturb them. "But now that they are asleep, I don't feel it so much."

Joseph nodded. "Are you still craving sugar?"

Abbie considered his question. She looked down at the flat bread. "No."

"Okay, let me get dinner cooked and get you fed, hopefully before they wake up. Then we need to talk about their effect on you." He paused. "And me."

"I don't think they intend me harm."

"No, I don't either. I'm just concerned… since we don't really know much about them."

Abbie nodded, looking at the sleeping bodies all over the interior of the little house. "Yeah, we should talk."

Chapter Ten

"Mmm. This was so good. What were those hamburger patties made with? Ground lamb and…" Abbie dipped a piece of flat bread in the hummus and put it in her mouth. She perched on a stool at the tiny bar, beside Joseph. The faeries continued to sleep.

Joseph chuckled. "First of all, they were not hamburger patties. They were kibbeh. It's a Lebanese dish my grandmother always made. *She* made them with lamb, which is hard to find in Loville, but if you ask at the meat counter…" He shrugged.

Abbie laughed. "So that smooth-as-silk accent works on other people, too." Then she looked at the faeries. Gosh. She'd forgotten they were asleep. "Shh."

"And this—?" She held up the flat bread as she whispered.

"Also Lebanese. It's called mountain bread."

She nodded, pointing with her little finger because her thumb and the first fingers held another piece of mountain bread. "Bean salad. But it taste different from what my mom makes."

"Right. It's a Lebanese recipe, too. Fava beans, chickpeas, and white beans, a little parsley, olive oil, garlic, and lemon juice, It's supposed to marinate in the refrigerator for a few hours, but I rushed it. Another secret from Abuela." He touched her forehead with his. "It'll be better tomorrow."

"Mums the word. Your abuela will never hear anything from me." She crossed her heart with an index finger. "So… all these Lebanese dishes, and yet you obviously speak Spanish?"

He smiled. His white teeth glistened. Abbie stared at the one canine turned slightly out of alignment with the others. It was adorable.

"Well, we speak Lebanese too, but yes. I am third generation, full-blood Lebanese. My great-grandfather came to Mexico a long time ago and since then, we have all been born in Monterrey."

"Oh, wow. But your English is so good."

He nodded. "I graduated from high school when I was fifteen. I suppose my exceptional marks caught the attention of a professor in Texas, who gathered students under his arms."

Abbie chuckled. "You mean wings. He gathered students under his wings. Like a hen gather's her chicks all safe and sound under her wings."

"Yes. Wings. He issued me a scholarship that included housing and a food allowance. I got my Bachelors in three years, skipped the Masters, under his guidance, and obtained my PhD in Chemical Physics over the next three years. I visit Monterrey a lot, but I have lived in the United States ever since."

"Ah." Abbie tipped her head back and dropped another piece of mountain bread into her mouth. "That explains a lot."

"What about you?" Joseph scooped a fork full of beans into his mouth and chewed.

"Me? Oh, I've always been fascinated with rocks. My mother said I was more like a boy than a girl. She constantly found rocks in the wash, because I had gathered them and didn't take them out of my pockets before giving her my laundry." Abbie laughed, then cringed.

"Shhh." She and Joseph whispered at the same time.

"When I graduated high school, there was no question what I'd major in when I went to college. Karole was already on a fast-track to medical school. I went for geology. I loved it so much, I just kept going until I had a PhD and they made me go get a real job." She giggled, then sat up straighter. "I also minored in a form of physics that made me a candidate for the VEIL project. Who knew? I went that route because a professor friend of mine told me that a Geology degree alone was only going to land me in a classroom, or a mining operation. He suggested physics for diversity." Abbie laughed. "I'm sure glad I followed his advice. I love what I do!"

"It shows." Joseph stared into her eyes. She stilled under his sultry gaze. He leaned closer to her. His eyes darted from her eyes to her lips.

Her heart pounded in her ears as her breath quickened. She wanted him to kiss her. Suddenly, she thought of the spices in the food, the garlic, the hummus. "Wait!"

She leapt off the stool, covering her mouth with her fingers. "Let me go brush my teeth."

He chuckled, straightening his back. "Yes. We probably should clean up a bit." He stood next to his stool and carried their plates to the sink. He ran hot water and added dish soap. "You go do what you need to. I'll wash dishes."

"No." Abbie took a step toward him. What was wrong with her? Why did she stop him from kissing her? "Leave them. I have a rule. The cook doesn't clean up."

His eyebrows rose on his forehead. His white teeth shown with a wide smile. "Oh, well, I'm not one to break the rules."

"Really?" Abbie teased. "Well, then, I have another rule. Abbie is allowed to brush her teeth before you kiss her."

He laughed. "Then hurry back. That kiss is waiting for

you."

She turned with a giggle and rushed to the bathroom. She fumbled with the toothpaste, squeezing it too quickly onto her toothbrush, it fell into the sink. She groaned and applied another, lesser, amount and turned on the water. She brushed as quickly but thoroughly as she could, then wiped her mouth. Applied some lip gloss and ran her fingers through her hair. After housing over a dozen faeries, it was a hopeless mess, but she tried to put it in order. She turned right and then left. If only she had changed clothes while he was gone to the grocery store. Oh well…

She entered the living room. Joseph was sitting on the floor, next to the doll house. He looked up at her. Placed a finger in front of his lips. "Shhh." They are starting to wake up.

She looked inside. A few faeries sat up, others still reclined. But they were definitely waking. Disappointment washed over her. Did this mean she wouldn't get that kiss? She sighed and sat beside him on the floor.

She exaggerated a smiled, demonstrating the cleanness of her teeth. He looked at them, as if inspecting her work. "*Muy bien.*"

"Muchas gracias." She giggled.

He feigned surprise. "*¿Hablas español?*"

"No. But who doesn't know 'thank you' in at least five different languages? Around here anyway."

"You have a point. There are a lot of eggheads around here."

They laughed. His mirth faded as his eyes gazed into hers. Her breath caught as her heart sped up to a rate that couldn't be healthy. But who cared? She leaned toward him, as he moved closer to her. Their lips touched gently, like a rose petals at first. Joseph touched her back, pulling her closer, his kiss deepened. She melded into him.

Suddenly, panic washed over her. She sat up straight. Her eyes darted all over his face. "I- I'm sorry." She stood.

Joseph looked confused. "Did I do something wrong?"

"No. I- I don't know." In her peripheral the faeries took flight.

"Look at the prism stream." "They are aligning even more than before." "This is fascinating!" "Make them do it again!"

Abbie's heart filled with a desire she had never felt in her life. She wanted to pounce on Joseph. She stepped into his arms. "Kiss me again!"

He considered her, his face taut with uncertainty. "Are you sure?"

"Oh. You have no idea how sure I am." She pressed closer, tilting her head back, closed her eyes, and… waited. Anticipated. Ahh, she wanted him to kiss her!

At last, his soft, warm mouth touched hers. She pressed in harder, grabbing the back of his head, and digging her fingers into his thick hair. She devoured his mouth with such a savage rage. She wanted more! MORE! She shoved him back against the divan, but he slid out of her grasp. Her eyes flew open. What was wrong?

He looked at her with a furrowed brow.

"What- what's wrong?"

"Abbie. I don't think this is you."

"What do you mean? Of course it's me. Look, I'm standing right here! Please, let's do this!"

He glanced at the faeries. They all hovered above the doll house. Their faces were filled with enthralled excitement. Joseph stepped back. "No. It's not. It's them. They are doing this… to you… to us."

The swarm lowered slightly, as if they shrugged in flight as one entity. "Look at them, Abbie. They are way too invested in being right there, beside you. They are pressing these emotions into you. I don't know how, but they are. Just like when they first came out of the fog. They did this to me, only it was different. They made me paranoid and angry. It was all of a sudden, and I didn't realize it wasn't my own feelings. But now…" He leveled his eyes with hers. "Now, I'm certain. They affect our emotions, our feelings."

"You don't want to be with me?" Tears sprang into Abbie's eyes.

"No, that's not what I'm saying." He jammed his fingers into his hair, pulling it back over his head. "I do want to be with you. But not like this. I really think these creatures are so fascinated with… love. It's a new discovery to them, and they are manipulating us to demonstrate the act of love… for their amusement. Do you get what I'm saying?"

His eyes roved over her. "Yes, I am intrigued by you. I want to get to know you better. But they are affecting what we feel and causing us to move way faster than I would ever —"

Abbie stared at him. Giggles trickled from the faeries beside her. A fog of confusion swamped her brain. She knew what she felt, she wanted him. Here and now! Like she'd never wanted anybody, ever before!

Ever before?

Wait. She'd never moved so fast on a guy. Dr. Joseph Assad piqued her interest from across the cafeteria. She'd spoken to him for the first time just this morning… and she really liked him, but what she felt now… this was pure lust. She shook her head, as if to shake the fog from her mind. This wasn't the way she acted. She had better control of her faculties than this. She was disciplined!

She staggered back. The faeries swooped with her. "It is *your* prism stream."

Her hands came up without thought, she swatted them back. Some of them cried out in pain. Her heart clenched. She didn't mean to hurt them. "I'm sorry." She looked directly at the swarm. "Please, get back from me."

They followed her movement. "We not hurt you." "We press more." "What you already feel." "We love the love."

"Please." She covered her face with her arms. "Stop… doing whatever you're doing to me… to Joseph."

Another step back, she stumbled against an end table. The corner hurt her thigh. "Quit!"

"We love watching your love." "It's fascinating."

Joseph quickly approached Abbie, steadying her from falling over the table.

Her leg hurt. Her heart hurt worse. "You're invading our privacy!"

The faeries continued. "Mother Righteous does not control you here." "You can love him." "All you want."

Abbie let him hold her. Leaning against his strength, she continued to face the swarm. "No, you don't understand. We *control* our emotions. There are rules. Etiquette. Appropriate behavior."

"But your prism streams align." "It is you who has love for him." "We are not—"

"STOP IT! Now!" Abbie staggered back from Joseph and the faeries.

They gasped in unison. Shocked, they hovered in the air, then fluttered back from her. "We are not hurting you." "Why do you not want your prism stream to align?"

Abbie search her mind. How could she make them

understand? "I-we want it to happen naturally. It's not right for you to force it to happen so fast. We need time. To- to learn about each other. You pressing our emotions is wrong."

The swarm gasped again. "Wrong?" "Mother Righteous hates love energy." "She forces us to smash it." "Your world is different." "How is pressing love wrong?"

Abbie groaned. "Because…" She turned to Joseph. Pleading silently for his help. He turned to the faeries. "Because love and joy and happiness happen in our world without faeries influencing it. You're right that this *mother righteous* doesn't affect our world, but that doesn't make it right for you to affect it even though you're working from the opposite direction."

The faeries hovered in front of Abbie and Joseph. They blinked. Their tiny mouths hung open. A wave of repentance washed over Abbie, but she held her ground, drawing strength from Joseph's closeness.

Aura fluttered out of the swarm. "We sorry."

The other's repeated her words.

"But." Aura trembled, clasping her hands around her middle. "But we cannot go back to Velona. We were secretly gathering those who did not agree with Mother Righteous. Her ways are frightening. We think she suspected it was us who gathered rebellious minds. She sent us out to test us.

"Soon we would have enough to come against her. It's

why we were so far from her mountain. We were afraid to be near her. She sensed our truth. Her hate is strong. Then your world went Boom! We knew it was our chance to be free.

"If we go back… Mother Righteous will… wipe our life like she did to Anak. There is nothing left of his life except the colors of his emotions."

Abbie glanced at Joseph then back to Aura. "I'm not saying you have to go back to your world. I don't know how, but we can learn to live in harmony with each other. You're a new discovery to us, and I guess, in a way, we are a new discovery to you. We should study our differences and similarities. Learn more about each other. But—"

"What?" Aura flew closer to Abbie.

"I don't know how to report that you are here without endangering you. My people are… they don't handle new life forms very well. Give me time to figure out what to do. And—"

Abbie moved to the stool at the bar and sat down. "Just… please stop forcing your… fascinations on us. Separate yourselves from me… and Joseph."

Aura's eyes flitted around the room. "Let you have your privacy."

Abbie smiled. "Yes. Everyone needs privacy."

"Not me." The faeries all spoke, but this time, they didn't say it in unison.

"Well. That's fine." Joseph responded gently. "But we humans do."

Chapter Eleven

Abbie walked across the VEIL grounds. The morning insects sang with the rising sun, crisp cool air chilled her skin, and a beautiful blushing sky made a picture-perfect backdrop.

All in drastic contrast to her sullen mood.

Angered by an early automated call on her cell phone which woke her from what little sleep she had managed. Fatigue saturated her limbs, making them fell much heavier than they should. She trudged toward Director Stettler's office, trying to let the foul mood dissipate. A team had been called to meet with the director. Staying in an on-site apartment made it convenient when a demand came to join a mandatory meeting with barely forty minutes to spare. She showered, applied some light make-up, and dressed in her normal attire for work. Now all she had to do was walk across the facility grounds.

Now she understood Holly Teak's brilliance in living on-site.

An odd sensation remained with her. The faeries had

agreed to remain in the apartment, in their new home Joseph had bought for them. And yet, Abbie worried about their safety.

The absence of all the faeries affected Abbie more than she could have imagined. She'd met them less than twenty-four hours ago, but without the mass of faeries, she felt disoriented, as if she had been forced to switch to her left hand and expected to function like normal. How could such an unusual change affect her so deeply so soon?

Pausing to pour herself a coffee from the table just outside the director's office, Abbie looked up the hall. How odd for Stettler to have a hospitality table here. What strange etiquette for the man who typically presented himself as an irate drill sergeant. Did the event in Lab One humanize him somehow? Abbie mused. Or was it Melissa, his secretary?

She thumped a sugar package, then tore the top edge.

"Good morning." She lifted her eyes to the sultry Hispanic accent. Joseph's voice warmed her insides better than any amount of hot coffee ever could.

"Good morning."

"You get much sleep?"

"Not really. About the time I drifted off, my phone woke me and here I am."

Joseph chuckled. "Me too." He perused her head. "Where is everyone?"

Abbie sighed, keeping her voice low so that only Joseph could hear. "Our discussion last night convinced them to try some independence.

Joseph nodded. Pressing a lid on his coffee travel cup, he placed his hand on Abbie's back to guide her into Stettler's office. She nearly rose to her tip-toes, but forced herself to walk as if unaffected by his touch.

The Director sat perched on the corner of his desk, as if to portray a casual briefing was about to take place. Joseph and Abbie sat in an obviously borrowed chair and waited for the rest. An eclectic assortment of department representatives filled the room. Some had to stand. Abbie closed her eyes. Crowded offices were her greatest weakness. If only she could hold Joseph's hand to draw strength and calm her claustrophobia. She focused on sipping her coffee and counted backward by threes.

Attendees made eye contact with Abbie and Joseph, but few said more than, "Morning." Stettler remained silent, his arms crossed over his chest, his eyes following everyone as they walked in, then he'd simply stare at the door until the next person entered. A frown remained on his face when he began the meeting.

"Well, not everyone is here yet, but we need to get started." He scanned each face as if mentally taking roll. "All of you are aware of what happened yesterday. I've called you together this morning as a team. This team is vital to a successful investigation into this event. Now, what I expect from each of you is—"

Axel Ashton rushed into the room.

"'Bout time, Ashton." Stettler seemed to relax. Was this the last of the team to arrive?

"Dr. Crossan—"

Abbie straightened her back and focused on him.

"You tried to raise the alarm and no one listened. I apologize."

Whoa. Abbie didn't see that coming! Even though his tone didn't sound sincerely regretful, the fact that he said the words, in front of these key people, was saying a lot.

Stettler remained focused on her. "Do you have any additional theories as to what happened?"

Who? Me? Abbie blinked. He was focusing on her first? Not the chemical physicists who built the giant crystal, or Joseph who put pen to all the calculations that came out of Teak's pretty little head, or Axel Ashton, for that matter, who built all the equipment?

Where was Holly Teak anyway? Abbie glanced around one more time. Had she missed the woman? Surely she would be called in to help determine what went wrong and what the consequential effects were.

"Well, I- uh, only that the lab wall was damaged in the explosion. I can only assume the photon entanglement cascaded into the quartz crystals of the mountain. " She closed her mouth, and then opened it again.

She wanted to say, *But I look forward to investigating that very thing.* But Stettler jerked a nod and began speaking again. "I want you in there, extending your theory, testing. But not alone! No one goes in Lab One or near that wall alone. Partner up."

Abbie glanced at Joseph. *Partner up, check.*

"We need to know what the hell is happening with that fog, and for that matter, why we are getting fog in a dry mountain air."

Abbie opened her mouth to reply, but Stettler turned to Joseph. "Dr. Assad!"

She snapped her mouth closed with frustration. She couldn't wait to get started running tests. But where was Holly? Comparing current readings of the quartz wall around Lab One to Abbie's previous findings might yield information that could explain the dimensional opening. Holly was a key person for discussing that data. She knew the most about that man-made crystal in the center of the toroid and… Abbie considered Joseph.

He stiffened and responded to Stettler. The director went on. Specific orders were given— Investigate the side effects of that crystal. Why ask Joseph to do that? Why not Holly? She grew the darn thing. He knew her equations and anticipated results, but Abbie preferred to have this discussion with the one whose brain thought it up in the first place.

In fact, why were all these other people here? The only people needed for this team would be herself, Holly, Joseph and Axel. How could anybody else have any idea what went wrong or what to do about it?

Stettler moved his attention to the head of security, Sebastian Stone. At least his scrutiny was off of Abbie.

Yes, there was a lot to be learned from yesterday's event. One of which would be to recognize that there were creatures who had *infiltrated* our world. The large cumbersome thing had not been found, as far as she knew. She only knew about the faeries, but she was not naïve, if these two species made it through, there had to be more. Second, these fantastical creatures were living, breathing entities who actually had escaped a tyrannically oppressive leader. Her faeries were seeking political asylum here in this world, what else came through or why she had no clue, but could only assume they would be seeking the same new life. Could Stettler really handle such information? Without being the oppressive jerk that he was naturally and locking them up for further study.

Abbie waited for Stettler to pause, or ask if there was anything else. She wanted to give her opinion about diplomacy, potential alien life forms, a new species discovery. Maybe more…

But Stettler mentioned the tech who disappeared in the

explosion. Zeke Callahan.

Poor Zeke!

Stettler tasked everyone in the room to figure out what happened to him. His fiancé deserved an answer.

Fiancé? That's right. Joseph had mentioned Zeke had asked Amelia to marry him just the night before the accident. Well, yes, she sure did deserve an answer. We all did. Sadness deflated Abbie's ire. Maybe when she could get in to Lab One and examine that wall, she could find something that would indicate where Zeke went. It only stood to reason that if these other-worldly beings came here, perhaps Zeke went there. Could it be that simple? She imagined walking up to the quartz wall and sticking her hand through, into their world. Like in Stargate. Would it feel cold and fluidy?

Man! Abbie itched to get to work examining that wall!

A niggling, unwanted thought whispered at the back of her mind. Zeke could have imploded with the crystal. She winced, shrugging the offensive thought aside. Surely there would have been pink mist, something of his DNA, if that were the case. Abbie crossed her fingers at her side and sincerely hoping that was not the case. At least if Zeke got sucked into that other world, there was the possibility that he could be found and brought back.

"Lieutenant Stone, Dorothy; stick around." Stettler's bark brought Abbie's mind back to the meeting. "Everyone else, dismissed."

Dismissed.

Abbie stood. Numb from what she'd heard Stettler say. Bothered by her own indecisive thoughts. Forgotten was her two-cents worth that she had wanted to interject. She followed the team out into the hall. Could she and Joseph go straight to the Lab and get started? She leaned close to Joseph's ear. "Where's Dr. Teak?"

"I have no idea." Joseph looked around for good measure. "You suppose Stettler is blaming her for the accident?"

Abbie shrugged. "Why? It only makes sense to me that she'd be part of this team. She knows more about that entanglement machine than any of us... well, except you, of course... and Axel, since he built it."

"No, you're right. It's all her... brain baby. What did you call it?"

Abbie giggled. "Brain child."

"Right. Brain child. I just verified her equations. She came up with the formulas."

"Yeah. So why isn't she here?"

Axel Ashton joined them walking away from Stettler's office. "Because Stettler deems her unreliable, whatever that means. He's restricted her from the physics building, her office, and the labs. He even took her computer and cell phone. Can you believe that?"

"He just confiscated it from her? Why?"

Axel shrugged. "Well, he let her voluntarily turn them over to his security guys. But what choice did she have? If she refused, it makes her look guilty of … something. I don't know."

"So… " Abbie considered Axel's comment. "If Stettler doesn't want anyone to talk to her, and doesn't consider her objective or reliable—" Abbie shook her head. "I just don't get it. What does any of that mean?"

"I don't know." Axel jammed his hands in his pockets and continued to walk with them.

"Hmm." Abbie touched his arm drawing him back. "As you just heard, I've actually been *ordered* to work in there, to find out what the heck happened."

Axel nodded.

"Look." Abbie continued. "I'll do everything I can to figure out my end of this dilemma. But I can't see us actually resolving much without Holly's input." She looked over her shoulder. They stepped outside the building and walked down the crushed granite walk through the indigenous garden. Abbie checked all around them. "Maybe when we need to know something that only Holly would know, you could get our question to her and…"

Axel brightened. "Yeah. Maybe we can work with her that way."

"Right." Abbie smiled.

Axel looked worried and relieved at the same time. "Well, thank you Abbie. I know you and Holly haven't always seen eye to eye. But none of this is her fault." He ran his hand through his hair. "I really appreciate you… helping figure this out."

Abbie pursed her lips. Remorse swept through her heart. She had never really given Holly a chance. She was a genius, just like Joseph. Maybe more than Joseph. Obviously, Axel had strong feeling for her, and those feelings weren't wrapped up in her brilliance for chemical physics. That, Abbie could relate to!

"I'm happy to help. Especially if Stettler is shutting her out. That really doesn't make any sense to me."

Axel shrugged. "Me neither."

"Yeah. I just need to run by my temporary apartment for one thing." Abbie smiled sympathetically at Axel and glanced at Joseph. Joseph nodded, he understood what she was about to do, and pulled away from Axel to walk with her. Axel dropped his eyes to the ground and solemnly walked toward the QEPL. "So, I'll see you at Lab One?"

Abbie and Joseph nodded.

"Yep. Axel's in love with Dr. Teak."

"What makes you say that?" Joseph side-stepped from her to level his eyes with hers.

"Are you kidding? It's as obvious as…" Abbie looked around. "As fifteen obvious things." She waggled her eyebrows.

Joseph frowned. "Let's not talk about that out here."

Abbie continued her thought. "All the more reason to get this figured out and, hopefully, resolved. For *everybody*." Abbie touched her hair. Sensing the faeries absence. Did the faeries have anything to do with all these new relationships popping up all of a sudden?

A residual jealous sensation pierced Abbie's heart. She and Joseph were getting to be pretty close. How long had Holly and Axel been seeing each other? They worked nearly twenty-four-seven. Maybe they'd kindled their relationship *while* working together. That was something Abbie and Joseph didn't have. Until now. Now, they were *partnered up*, ordered to work together. What a delightful outcome to a tragic event. Abbie's shoulders rounded. She bit her bottom lip. How selfish.

"Well, okay." Abbie shook off the compunction. "Lets go get the faeries and examine a quartz wall." Abbie stepped more lively.

Joseph took her elbow, stopping her. "You think that's wise?"

"Something tells me these faeries are vital to our investigation. Besides, what could it hurt?"

Joseph frowned. "Exactly my point."

Chapter Twelve

Abbie stood in the fog with Joseph in Lab One. It was like being in a steam room. The mist gave the impression of heat, but the wall was cool to the touch. The fragrant floral aroma of a tropical jungle wafted through the fissure. Abbie made a mental note to bring a fan next time. Surely they could move this mist out to the woods where it would dissipate in the dry mountain air.

The faeries had refused to go with her to the wall. They insisted they should remain in their tiny house inside her temporary apartment. Why they were so terrified of the wall was unclear, but she didn't have the heart to force them to come, even if they could be valuable in explaining how they came through. She had drawn the curtains and locked the door.

Worry lingered in her heart that someone might come in the apartment and they would be found. She had warned them to stay hidden if anyone other than Joseph, Karole, or herself walked into the apartment. The term, "stranger-danger" meant so much more for them, considering if anybody among the VEIL facility guards or scientists found any form of alien beings in her apartment. They'd become lab rats in a split second.

The large creature that emerged from the fog yesterday still hadn't been found, nor had any trace of it been seen. That was so odd. She patted the wall. It was solid as a … well, as a rock. Unless its chemical compound had changed immediately after the accident, she couldn't see how the creature would have returned otherwise. But anything was possible.

Abbie chipped pieces away from the scintillating quartz wall. "You know." She spoke softly to Joseph. "If only the faeries weren't so afraid, I'd have brought them here to help determine what was going on with these flickering lights."

Joseph frowned. "Abbie. It's not like you can carry them across the compound. They are not chihuahuas."

"I know, you're right, but what do they think will happen? Mother Righteous will reach through and grab them?" Abbie chuckled. "Perhaps she would? They know this ruling gorgon, we don't."

"I'm sure they are right to be so cautious." Joseph marked a container before lifting it to where she chiseled pieces of quartz. "You should be more cautious, too."

"Well, I'd love to get their input on the content of the samples. Does it exist on their side too? Maybe we could bring some samples back to the apartment tonight." A queasy sensation lingered, distracting her from her fact gathering. She leaned back to examine the wall. An oval darkness filled the pink opacity, making it almost purple.

She paused to consider the variation in the rock.

"Hmm." A theory formed in her head. Would the component that caused the quartz to flicker with colored lights remain once the rock was removed from the wall? That was something she'd prove, or disprove, in just a moment when she loosened some of the quartz where the scintillation effect lingered.

Any changes from before the accident would be catalogued along with any changes from this sampling today. This color variance couldn't be compared to anything since the building was constructed but she did have samples from when the mountain was excavated before construction.

Her gaze remained on the rock she was about to chip away from the fissure, while she spoke to Joseph. "Please note these samples have lost that… twinkling lights affect as soon as I separated them from the larger mass."

Joseph jerked a nod as she placed the chunk into a container he held out for her.

Her eyelashes brushed against the safety glasses as she blinked. Condensation obscured her view of his ruggedly handsome face.

Joseph marked the container on a white painted area,

like a label, with a special pen, designating where the samplings were taken and wrote corresponding information on a chart attached to a clipboard.

A loud metal-on-concrete noise startled Abbie. She gasped and jumped, nearly dropping her chisel. She had forgotten Axel and Rick Sharp were working in the lab also. Had they heard anything Abbie and Joseph had said about the faeries?

Orange plastic strings draped behind their necks which told her they did not. They were wearing earplugs.

Stettler had assigned Axel and Rick to build a containment cage. They were organizing assorted metal pieces and mesh wiring that had been delivered this morning. At least it proved that Stettler acknowledged the big creature had come through the wall. Anybody else on-site who spoke of the incident swore it was just a bear. That thing was way bigger than just a bear. The phrase had become so prevalent she heard that The Oasis had a dark stout beer with whipped cream on top labeled "Just-a-Beer."

A hand-drawn sketch of the cage lay on a desk under the observation area. Axel and Rick worked far away from Abbie and Joseph assembling the basic framework. Soon, Abbie would have to be finished collecting her samples because the cage would be placed up against the twinkly lit wall. The assumption being this was where additional creatures would come through.

Joseph lifted another beaker from a rolling cart they had brought from her office and set near the study sight. He held the glass jar under Abbie's chisel.

They wiped their safety goggles against their lab coat sleeves and kept working. The dancing lights were so distracting they both paused to take in the spectacle. Distorted shapes beyond the quartz were visible too. Abbie looked closer at the strange muted image. Joseph leaned toward the distortions. "What is that?"

"I have no idea." Abbie smiled resolutely at him. "From the smell, I'd say foliage. It wasn't there before this building was built, I can assure you. Before this facility was built, it was my assignment to study this entire mountain. I have documentation that it was solid quartz. That was *the* reason the facility was built into this elevation. Now, and only in this specific area of the wall, it looks like an opaque window to a garden… or something. What I find really strange, it this darkened rock. It's almost like—"

She moved to the slit where the quartz seemed to be separating along a cleavage. For good measure, Abbie changed her safety glasses for a special UV set and lifted a special light. "No traces of blood."

Joseph nodded. "So, no sign Zeke was sucked through."

"Right." She switched back to the clear googles and scraped chunks of purpling quartz into a separate glass container. Now that it was separate from the wall, it appeared to be the lighter pink. "What I was saying, is I don't understand this purpling effect."

He marked the jar and lifted another.

"One of the things I'll be checking for is fibers when we get back to my lab." Abbie concentrated on the fissure rocks. The gap was just wide enough to get a glimpse of the world invoked by this entanglement.

Joseph pursed his lips. So far there had been nothing to indicate what had happened to the tech. Fibers or blood would indicate Zeke's body had been sucked through this sliver of a crack in the quartz, which would also indicate he was dead.

Abbie paused in her chipping, staring through the slight crack. She could make out lush green foliage, ferns perhaps, white, yellow, and red blooming shoots, bugs or maybe birds singing to one another. It was a tropical paradise—

A large, orange, snake-like eye popped in front of the opening.

"Ahhh!" Abbie fell back from the wall, panting. Her heart pounded in her chest. Joseph started, dropping the glass container. It shattered. The figure vanished.

"What was that?" Abbie spoke louder than she had intended. She angled her head to look again, but the figure was beyond her visual range. Nausea roiled in her gut. She swallowed against it. Whatever or whoever that was, it seemed to be gone now. Perhaps she'd scared it as much as it scared her.

She turned to Joseph with wide eyes, concentrating on steadying her breathing.

"Are you alright?" Joseph stepped closer to her. "Maybe we should take a break."

Abbie shook her head. "No, I'm alright. It just surprised me. As beautiful as it appears to be over there, I'm pretty sure it's an illusion." Abbie touched her collar bone, calming her breathing and her heart. "It's gone now. Let's keep working."

Joseph nodded, but he didn't look as though he agreed.

Abbie turned to retrieve a drill and two sets of ear-protection headphones. Joseph took one set while she placed the other over her ears.

Abbie's attention moved to the broken toroid. Tattooed burn marks darkened the floor. Ram-set bolts lay bent and severed where the power coupling had been. Who removed it? Where had it been taken? Was someone examining it for evidence of what might have caused the accident? Axel had built the thing, why hadn't he been assigned to examine it? Stettler's orders made less and less sense.

She drew in a deep breath, bringing her gaze back to Ashton and Sharp. "This is going to be loud!"

Ashton and Sharp ignored her. She shrugged. If they

hadn't heard her yell that the drill would be loud, they certainly didn't hear her speaking quietly about the faeries.

Abbie placed the hole saw against the less illuminated quartz and pulled the trigger. She cut a shallow core sample. Removing the sample disk from the saw, she marked it with a sharpie, placed it on the table, and moved twelve inches toward the fissure and the twinkly-lit area. She couldn't help but to glance through the fissure before starting the drill. With no frightening figure, only abundant greenery seen, she drilled another sample, marked it, and moved further along the wall.

The ominous feeling tiptoed across her skin despite the absence of any evidence to warrant the sensation. This work had to be done. She was the one to do it, so she suppressed her instincts to stay away from this wall and kept drilling. Joseph's presence helped calmed her nerves and made her feel safe.

After a while, she had a line of shallow holes all the way across and above the fissure. She removed her ear protection. "I wonder?"

Abbie walked to the desk where her assorted tools were and retrieved a metric ruler from her canvas tool bag. Joseph stayed near the wall but watched her return. She shamelessly put a little extra swing in her step as she approached him.

A sensation of warmth radiated through her body. The

heat crept up her neck and filled her cheeks. She liked having Joseph here with her. Stettler had demanded everyone work in pairs. Which would have been a nuisance, if she weren't so attracted to this particular Chemistry Physicist.

She glanced at Ashton. The poor sucker got stuck with a security guard. Although he seemed to know what he was doing as they worked out a strategy to create some sort of containment cage.

Her eyes drifted to Joseph. She grinned at him. His lips parted and his gleaming white teeth showed through as he returned her smile. A desire to put everything down and just kiss him coursed through her veins. She cleared her throat instead and turned back to the cracked wall.

Placing the metal ruler across the darkened split in the quartz, she measured the width of the crack along the fissure from point to point. Twelve measurements. She'd do this every day until the cage prevented her from standing this close. She spoke the readings to Joseph. He recorded each measurement with an arrow pointing at the approximate place on a penciled drawing of the opening he had sketched for her on graph paper.

Together they gathered samples, while Ashton built his contraption, until a voice from the hall announced the lunch cart was here. Abbie looked at her watch. "Wow. It's already four o'clock."

The four of them grabbed sandwiches, chips and drinks from the cart and returned to their work. Abbie asked for a peanut butter and honey sandwich. She would save it for the faeries.

She continued taking samples and recording measurements until the exterior light pouring in from the exposed woods faded. Abbie yawned.

"Let me walk you to your apartment." Joseph put away his goggles and helped her gather her tools into the canvas tool bag.

"Let's take all these samples back to my office first. I'll run tests first thing tomorrow."

Joseph agreed. Abbie gathered her canvas tool bag, while Joseph carefully covered the roller cart with a canvas tarp.

Abbie approached Axel before walking out of Lab One. She touched his shoulder, and he pulled his earplugs from his ears. "How's Holly holding up?"

Axel shrugged. "I stopped by her apartment before coming here, but she wasn't there. I haven't had a chance to catch up with her since."

Abbie nodded. Her heart ached for the woman. Even though she seemed obnoxious, Abbie understood the need to get ones hands on an experiment that went wrong and figure out what happened. She truly could imagine how beside herself Holly must be right now. "Surely Stettler will let her follow up on the accident."

Axel lifted an eyebrow. Doubt filled his face. "You'd think."

Abbie wanted to tell him everything would work out. But something was off about Stettler and his decision to ban Holly from this investigative team. She pursed an empathetic smile instead and walked out with Joseph pushing her cart.

Maybe tomorrow truly would be another day.

Joseph knocked on Abbie's door just as she opened it. His eyes widened. "Oh. You're ready?"

She backed up and picked up the doll house. The open side was covered by a pillow case tacked to the roof. She turned the covered side toward her chest. "I am now."

Joseph looked at Abbie sternly. "You're taking the faeries?"

"Yes. I believe their knowledge of crystals will be beneficial to our investigation."

"And you're thinking you can carry them across the facility in the doll house without bringing up any suspicions?" Joseph blocked her leaving the apartment.

"I'm not taking them to the Quantum Labs, just my

office. We don't have to go through security checkpoints. If anyone asks, I'll tell them you and I are fixing this up for my… little cousin."

Joseph didn't move. "We could bring the samples you collected yesterday back here."

"Yeah, but that'll be tonight. I really want to get answers today." Abbie shifted the house. Its weight beginning to feel heavier.

"So… taking them to your office will speed up your investigation?"

"That's the plan." Abbie took a step toward him, hoping he'd step aside. "Can you stay and help? I'll bring them back here if we go to Lab One again. I do want to measure that fissure again before sundown. And before Axel and Rick get that cage in place."

"Honestly, with Dr. Teak restricted, I might as well help you as to tweet my thumbs in my lab. But it concerns me to move the faeries across the facility."

Abbie laughed. "You mean twiddle, twiddle your thumbs."

Joseph chuckled. "Yes. That's what I mean."

"Good. I like having you around." Abbie grinned mischievously. "I only need to take them this one time. We'll be careful and once they are able to give me some feedback, I'll rush them back here."

"And I like being around you. I really think this is an

unnecessary risk. But—" Joseph took the doll house from her and walked into the hall. "I can see your mind is made up."

He led the way out of the building and through the indigenous garden. "Fall is definitely in the air. It feels chilly this morning."

"Brrr. Yes, it does. I should have brought my sweater."

"Do you want to go back and get it?" Joseph paused but he didn't look happy to go back.

"No, I can wear my lab coat if I am cold in my lab."

He nodded and continued toward the QuESO building. "I hope you're right about this."

Chapter Thirteen

While Abbie examined the core slices under the microscope, Joseph sketched out some equations on a smart pad. She'd tell him what to enter in her computer from her observations, and he'd comply, then return to his calculations. In the meantime, another computer sounded. Abbie glanced up from the scope. "Ah, good."

She walked to the screen and pushed two keys on the keyboard. A printer cranked out a report. She returned to the microscope and designated some more information for him to record. When the printer halted, Abbie retrieved the data and shuffled through the printouts.

"Hmm."

"Anything impressive?" Joseph craned his neck as if he could see her data sheets.

She glanced at him with baffled eyes. "No?"

He pursed his lips. "Hmm. I've run through some calculations before the experiment and even with the absence of the concrete wall, I still can't justify a quantum entanglement big enough to connect another dimension."

She turned to him. "If this accident was caused by entanglement gone wrong, or that crystal exploding, there'd be evidence of the crystal intrusion in the concrete, in the quartz wall, or … somewhere. The way the lab wall blew out and that instantaneous swoosh that took everything through the quartz, like an implosion… but the mountain wall looks unharmed, minus that fissure we measured— I just can't make sense of it." She paused. "Okay, maybe the faeries squeezed through that fissure, but that behemoth *thing* we saw… there's no way it stepped through that tiny crack. He *had to* just pass through that quartz wall." She pierced him with questioning eyes. "None of this makes sense, Joseph."

He tilted his head with a shrug. "Unless it *was* just a bear."

Abbie laughed. "That *thing* was *not* just a bear!"

They sobered. His eyes focused on nothing. His mind reeling with possibilities. "I wish we could examine that power coupling. I can't remember how it looked after the event. There was the window glass broken… debris from the lab wall crumbled, and that… fog… the crystal was… just gone… like Zeke, just vanished. But I can't remember what the power coupling looked like."

Abbie licked her lips in thought. "Neither do I." She turned to the faeries clustered on her desk against the opposite wall. She had assembled the rock samples she'd taken from around the fissure and laid them out for their inspection. She had spent an hour writing down everything they said about the samples. Nothing was unusual now that it was separate from the scintillating wall, or like what they had seen on their side.

"How did you come through from your side of the… to our world."

They looked at her curiously, blinking as if on cue. "We are not sure." "We heard a noise." "We flew near to see what it was." "A lot of… trash flew out at us." "Many colors." "Shapes." "Odd things." "We flew closer to see." "Next thing we knew…"

Aura stood out from the others. "We were here."

Abbie turned to her counter and lifted a pencil. She sketched out a drawing and lifted to toward the faeries. "Did you see anything that looked like this? Only it was about…" She put the paper down and held out her hands to show the size of Holly's crystal. "This big."

The faeries shook their heads.

Abbie lifted her eyes to Joseph. "So, if there is a portal… it must be, I don't know… active on their side? But why? And— is it the rock or the fog?"

Joseph squinted. "When we were outside, standing on the side of the mountain, the faeries came out of the fog. And the fog sparkled like the quartz wall does now." He paused. "I think the fog has something to do with it, but I don't think it's the portal. Did you take samples of it?"

"Yes." She turned to another computer. "Just a minute." She clicked several keys. Stared at the screen. Clicked some more keys, then refreshed the screen. "I don't get this."

She looked at Joseph. He walked over and peered over her shoulder. Abbie turned her head, intending to tell him her impressions. But a fragrance diverted her attention and she inhaled deeply.

He leaned into her. "RawChemistry."

"W-what?" She blinked.

"My cologne, it's called RawChemistry. One of my sisters bought it for me as a joke, but I like the fragrance." A blush flooded his face. "I take it you agree."

Abbie dropped her eyes and cleared her throat. "Yes. I do." She smiled. "So, anyway." She cleared her throat again. "The water samples, like everything else, don't make sense. I was expecting sulfuric acid, or something mineral based, organic, even. All we have is equivalent to distilled water."

"Really?"

Abbie looked at the screen and back to him. "Well…" She looked back at the read out. "Yes, really. Okay, there's a slight uptick here." She pointed at the chart. "But it's not enough to be conclusively mineral or organic."

"Hmm." Joseph straightened. "You know, we really can't dismiss anything as an expected anomaly. We don't know if the fog was sparkling or if it was just picking up the effect from the wall. After all, when we walked into the fog it did not sparkle around us. Only the wall sparkled. So it's… probably the wall.

"But there is something about that fog. It is different than any mist or steam I've ever seen. Nothing seems to affect its dissipation. And it seemed to move so far, then pull back, remember? Right after the… accident?"

She nodded, also in thought.

He rubbed the back of his neck and paced along the bank of computers. "You know, I personally wrote down and verified every one of Dr. Teak's calculations. She wasn't wrong."

He stared at Abbie. She returned his gaze. "I believe you. Although you guys were not taking into account the negative possibilities. Holly said she was assuming only the pos—" Abbie closed her eyes. "You know what? We've already been through that. All I'm saying is the composition of the quartz wall is far more complex than Holly's crystal. Indium, florine, chlorine, and traces of about fifteen other elements, including gold. There's no computer simulation powerful enough to determine how entanglement might manifest in that kind of a hodgepodge."

"And there's still the question of how the photons from Holly's crystal caused the lab wall to break which allowed the entangled photons to cascade into the quartz."

Abbie laid the printouts down and returned to her microscope. "How could that have happened?"

"A separate event? An implosion that punched a hole in the back of Lab One giving the photons direct access to the quartz?" Joseph shook his head. "Without looking at the power coupling or the crystal, we'll never know."

"Then we, or somebody needs to examine that power coupling." Abbie stared at Joseph.

"Right."

"So, now what?"

"You write up your report, submit it to the investigation team, and I'll find out who was assigned to examine the power box."

Abbie nodded. "And… let's go by to see how Holly is doing after we take the faeries back to my temporary apartment."

Joseph cocked his head back in surprise. "Okay? You having a change of heart toward Dr. Teak?"

"Maybe. I mean, times have changed and one of our own is being mistreated. We need to find out what her theory is."

"But she's restricted from her lab."

"You don't honestly think that will stop her from analyzing what happened? She's a genius. Besides, you said yourself, you put pen to her cognitive calculations. She doesn't have to be in her lab to review her calculations."

"You have a point. Let's go there now."

"Yes." Abbie shut down her computers, gathered her papers, stuffing them in a manila folder, and put it in her satchel. She pulled the satchel and her purse over her shoulder and stood beside Joseph. "Ready?"

He gestured for the faeries to climb into the doll house and reattached the pillow case to the open side. His eyes flitted between hers. "You know. I have to admit. Whether it's the faeries influence or not, I really like working with you, Dr. Crossan."

"Awwww." The faeries cooed from inside the house.

Abbie looked their way, then back to Joseph. She smiled. "I like working with you, too, Dr. Assad."

He wrapped his arm around her shoulder, drawing her closer to him. She closed her eyes. The warmth of her skin radiated against his face. His lips brushed lightly against hers. An exhilarating sensation washed through him—

"Um, excuse me." A young woman, wearing the sandwich vendor apron, pushed the sandwich cart into Abbie's office. The woman glanced back at the hall.

Abbie stumbled away from Joseph. Gasping for air.

The woman took another step, speaking softly. "Do you know where I can find Axel Ashton? I-I've got a sandwich order for him."

Joseph gawked at the woman. "Amelia?" He whispered. "Parker… isn't it? How did you get in here?"

The woman looked startled. "You're… Joseph… Abdul-Jabar?"

Abbie chuckled. The heat of embarrassment filled her cheeks. But this mystery woman calling Joseph Abdul-Jabar filled her heart with amusement, and yet, her instincts knew something was terribly wrong.

Joseph stepped away from Abbie. "Assad, actually. Come in here." Joseph rushed to her and pulled her into Abbie's office. He turned to Abbie. "This is Zeke Callahan's fiancée. I had a beer with Axel and Zeke in town a time or two. That's how I met her." He turned back to Amelia. "You're not supposed to be here. How did you get past security at the front gate?"

"Would you believe I bribed my friend, Casey Kim, to let me bring her sandwich cart from Java the Hut?"

Abbie's brows rose. *Resourceful.*

He closed his eyes and leaned his head back with a heavy sigh. "Oh, Amelia. You shouldn't be here."

"I need answers, Joseph! Where's Zeke?" she whispered.

Abbie started. Oh my goodness… She glanced at the doll house where her faeries hid from the intruder. *Don't move! Don't make a sound!* She hurried past Amelia to gently close her office door.

"Come sit down." Abbie guided her to a stool in the lab.

Tears filled Amelia's eyes. "They called me… the other night… and said there had been an *incident* in the lab." She lifted pleading eyes to Joseph.

He touched her shoulder as she spoke. She continued. "What kind of incident, Joseph? Is Zeke alright? Did he get hurt? They wouldn't tell me *any* details. I've been losing my mind ever since that phone call."

She sucked in air. "I called Medical. A, uh, Dr. Crossan wouldn't tell me anything other than Zeke was not there." She glanced at Abbie's lab coat. Anger and frustration filled her narrowed eyes. "Are you who I talked to?"

"No." Abbie reached to touch Amelia's arm. "My sister is a doctor in medical. You must have talked to her. But—"

"How could they call and tell me so little? Don't they realize not knowing exactly what happened would drive me more crazy than being honest with me? I have a really vivid imagination. My mind can make up way worse things than what probably is reality." She folded over, crying into her hands. "I just want to know what happened to my fiancé!"

Then she looked up and pierced Abbie with a sorrow filled glare. "Please, just tell me— is Zeke dead?"

"… We don't know." Abbie mumbled. Joseph shot a reprimanding look at her. She shrugged. "We don't. She deserves to know the truth."

Hope filled Amelia's face. "Yes, please! Tell me the truth."

Joseph drew in a deep sigh. "Everything that happened is classified top secret. We-we are under strict orders— but what they said to you *es verdad*— is true. There *was* an incident, and Zeke… *was* involved. We honestly do not know what happened to him." Joseph jammed his hand in his hair, his eyes darted across the floor as if the right thing to say was there somewhere.

"He… he just vanished." Joseph lifted his eyes to meet Amelia's. "That's all we know. But we are working diligently to figure out what went wrong and what happened." He turned to Abbie, as if presenting her. "This is Dr. Abbie Crossan. She's a geologist here. She and I have been tasked to investigate the… results of the incident."

Amelia leapt to her feet. "A geologist! Why would a geologist be needed to figure out what happened to my Zeke?" She shook her head vehemently. "I just don't understand!"

Joseph continued, easing her back onto the stool. "We have core samples and…" He glanced at Abbie. His eyes widened.

Then he turned back to his friend. "Amelia, go home!" he spoke gently. "Trust me. We are working on finding out what happened. I know it's hard to wait." He looked around and found a small spiral notepad. "Here, write down your number. I will personally call you the minute we know something."

Amelia stared at the pad. "If all this is classified, how can you—?" She turned to Abbie. "How could you not know?" As if in a trance, she lifted the pen and wrote her number. "How could he just disappear? Did he blow up into that pink mist? I saw that happen on *Scrubs*. This guy was carrying a bomb… and he… just… blew up."

Sobs heaved her forward. Her shoulders lurched. Just as suddenly, she gained composure and lifted her face. "Did he get blown into oblivion or something? What really happened?" Tears poured down her chapped cheeks.

Empathetic tears filled Abbie's eyes. "I'm sorry. We honestly don't— there was no pink mist. I promise."

Joseph glared at Abbie.

"Well! There wasn't. She deserves to at least know that!"

Joseph nodded. "Look, Amelia. You've got to go home. You cannot get caught impersonating the sandwich vendor. You'll get in big trouble. We don't want that. Go home. I swear on my grandmother's grave, I'll call you the minute I know something. In the meantime, have faith. We are doing everything we can to… get Zeke back."

"Back? Back from where?"

Abbie glared at Joseph. "I'm telling you. We don't know. That's all we can say about it. We're not keeping anything from you. We honestly DO NOT know where Zeke — what happened to Zeke."

Knuckles knocked on the lab door. "Dr. Crossan?"

The three jerked. Abbie sighed, "Oh no!"

"Dr. Crossan, it's Frank."

Abbie looked at Joseph. "What do we do?"

"Go answer the door." He turned to Amelia. "Be cool, stay calm."

She nodded, but worry filled her eyes.

Abbie opened her door. "Hey, Frank. What's up?"

"Is the sandwich vendor in there? I was on my way to QuIET Lake for a lunch break—"

"Yes, she's in here. Sorry, she's an old friend and we were just catching up."

Frank looked past Abbie to Amelia. "Sorry, ma'am. You're not allowed in the labs. You're supposed to stay in the halls." Concern wrinkled his brow. "Are you alright, ma'am?"

"Oh." Amelia slid off the stool, wiping her face with her sleeve. "I-I'm fine. We were just talking about old times. I get emotional."

Frank waited until she joined him in the hall. He bent to look at the shelves in her cart. "You got a corned beef on rye?"

"Yeah." She sniffed and cleared her throat. "I've got one of those." Fumbling through the bee's wrapped sandwiches, reading each label to find the right one, she handed Frank what he had asked for. "That'll be five dollars."

He handed her the bill and took the sandwich. "Thank you. Wait!" Frank considered her face. "I know you… you're the AT&T representative in town— hold on. You're Zeke Callahan's girlfriend! You can't be here, ma'am!"

Amelia's color drained from her face. Her knees buckled. Joseph rushed to catch her by the shoulders. "Take it easy, Frank." Joseph supported Amelia. "She's just desperate for answers. You would be too."

"Sure. But—" Frank looked her over. "She can't be here!"

"We know!" Abbie and Joseph said at the same time.

"Look." Frank took her arm. "Let me help you to your car. You leave the premises now and I won't report you were here."

She nodded. "Okay, but I have to take the cart. It belongs to Java the Hut."

"Fine. I'll help you take your cart, too. I'll report that the sandwich vendor… was ill and had to leave."

She nodded. Tears spilled over her lashes. "Okay. I'll go." She turned back to Joseph. "You promise?"

He jerked a nod. "You've got to trust me."

She sighed, stiffened her knees and back, and pushed her cart toward the front entrance of the QuESO building. A woman called out for a sandwich. Frank hollered over his shoulder. "Not now, Ling. She's not feeling well. Go to the cafeteria."

Abbie and Joseph watched as Frank walked with Amelia through the doors. Abbie turned to Joseph with wide eyes. "Poor Zeke!"

"Yeah. Let's get going. The sooner we figure this out, the sooner we can, maybe, get him home to her."

Chapter Fourteen

With the faeries safely delivered to Abbie's temporary apartment, she and Joseph leisurely strolled to the Quantum Labs building. Joseph took her hand and intertwined his fingers with hers. "What's on your investigative agenda this afternoon?"

"I really want to measure everything. The diameter of the scintillation, the width and length of the fissure, the volume of the fog."

Joseph nodded. "I think I'll take a look at what's left of the QuEST and measure the blast marks."

Abbie nodded. "Sounds like a good plan."

She smiled as she released his hand just as they entered the Quantum Lab Array Building. Sarge scanned their badges and exchanged their cell phones for a locker key. "Thank you, Sarge." Abbie slipped the keys in her pocket.

"More analyzing Lab One's incident?" Sarge's eyes filled with concern.

"Yes." Abbie shifted the tools bag on her shoulder. "I

want to see if anything has changed since yesterday. Are Ashton and Sharp still working on the containment cage?"

"Yep." Sarge scanned the floor. "I suppose it'll take a few days to complete that project."

Abbie walked a few steps. "We are counting on it taking some time, so I can get some more data from that wall before it's impossible to get up close."

Sarge saluted with two fingers. "Well, good luck, Doctors."

Joseph tipped his head back. "Thank you."

He led Abbie, although she knew the way now, to the back of the Labs Array. They presented their badges at the final entry checkpoint and entered Lab One. Axel and Rick, had the framework to the containment box assembled and were working on a gate. Abbie drew in a deep sigh. "Afternoon, gentlemen."

She crossed the lab floor, heading straight to the absent concrete wall. She sat her tool bag down on the ground and lifted the clipboard. She measured the features of concern while Joseph took out a carpenter's measuring tape and measured every scar and burn mark from the explosion.

Axel's drill and cutting saw filled the silent void as everyone worked at their own task. Abbie turned from the wall to consider the fog. Even with a box fan blowing into it, the fog did not dissipate. How odd. She took another sample of the moisture, then stood back from the mist to determine its size. "Joseph. Help me measure the height, width, and depth of this… fog."

"Sure." He zipped the carpenter's tape closed and walked to where she stood. Handing her the tip of the tape, he backed up from her. They both walked to what looked like the outer edge of the dense moisture. But every time she held her end of the measuring tape to what looked like the border of the fog, it seemed to contract away from her. "Hmm. I can't seem to get the exact outer measurement. Can you?"

"Well, no. It seems to be… undulating."

Abbie giggled. "That's a good way to describe it. Undulating fog. Just give me an approximation. It'll have to be good enough."

Joseph read her the measurement. She wrote it down and moved to measure the adjacent distance. Then she looked up toward the top of the mist. "You suppose we could get on a ladder to measure the height?"

Joseph craned his neck, I'd say its height changes just like its width, but I'd call that ten or twelve feet. What do you think, Ashton?"

Axel continued working. Joseph glanced at Abbie and pointed at his ears. Axel had earplugs in and couldn't hear them speaking. Abbie smiled and walked over to the Chief Mechanical Technician. She touched his shoulder. "Hey Axel."

He jerked and turned to see what she said. "Huh?" He pulled the orange cords from his ears.

"How high would you say that fog is?" Abbie pointed.

He looked over at the cloud of dense moisture. "Ten to twelve feet, I'd think."

Abbie chuckled. "Joseph said the same thing. Let's go with that. Would you say it changes? Like does it seem to be affected by us moving around in it or around it?"

Axel tilted his head. "You know, now that you mention it, I have noticed it… pulsing and… I don't know, maybe contracting when we are running the cutting tools. The fan doesn't seem to have any effect on it, at all."

Abbie nodded. "Interesting. I'll make note of that and if you see anything more unusual about the fog, will you let me know?" She pulled out a business card and wrote on the back of it, then handed him the card. "This is my cell phone number. If anything involving that wall or… whatever, in here, don't hesitate to call."

He nodded, but something in his eyes gave Abbie the impression he had something else to say. She waited, but he said nothing more. "Okay?"

"Sure." He glanced up.

She looked deep in his eyes, willing him to speak. His eyes darted toward Sharp. Ah. Maybe she could catch him outside of the lab and have this talk. She nodded and walked back to where Joseph stood. "So… now what?"

Joseph opened his mouth—

"How's it going in here?" Stettler strolled in. The four looked at him in surprise.

"Good." Joseph slipped the carpenter's tape into his pocket.

Stettler walked up to Abbie, but his cautious eyes remained on the fog and the scintillating wall sparkling through the dense vapors. "You getting enough data to give me an update, Doctors?"

"We'll have a written report for you tomorrow, Director." Abbie glanced at Joseph.

"Good. Listen, uh, Sheriff Spotted Wolf has been nosing around. I'm happy to work with her, but we got this under control, don't we?" Stettler glared at Joseph.

"Well, I—" Joseph glanced at Abbie. "I don't know, Director. We still can't tell you what happened to Callahan, and no one knows what happened to that big—"

"Ah." Stettler waved Joseph's response off. "I think we are safe to say that was just a bear."

Joseph stared at Stettler. "I think we all know it wasn't just a bear, but if that's what you want the public to think so there's no panic… I get it."

"Well, we gotta keep our business local to the site. What we got going on out here is on a need-to-know basis. And frankly, I don't think that sheriff needs-to-know. You understand what I'm saying?"

"Yes, Director." Joseph swallowed.

Stettler turned to Rick. "I know you two have been hard at this containment build, why don't you let me take over guarding the wall, you take a four or six hour break?"

Abbie's eyebrows lifted, but she resumed her placid expression. "Yeah, we were just finishing up, also. I'll have that report for you tomorrow before noon."

He nodded and turned back to Sharp and Ashton. "Come on. That's an order. You two take some time off and go get some rest."

Axel removed his safety goggles and put away his tools. Rick sluggishly wrapped electric cords around the power tools and set them against the far wall. Abbie glanced at Joseph. He moved a slight nod of affirmation.

She lifted her tool bag and joined Joseph at the door. "So, we'll see you gentlemen tomorrow."

"Oh." Stettler spun around to face her. "You have more to investigate?"

Abbie's eyes darted to Joseph's. "Well, I've been measuring a progressive and slight change in the… evidence."

"I see." Stettler puckered his lip in thought. "Well, I would think that is important. So how much change have you seen?"

"Some." Abbie lifted one eyebrow. "It'll all be in my report."

"Very well." Stettler turned his back on her. Essentially dismissing her and Joseph.

Joseph pulled her elbow. "Come on. Let's go have dinner."

"Yes. And I'd still like to go—" She glanced at Stettler. "To… that new restaurant in town. Talula's isn't it?"

"Great idea." Joseph pulled her into the hallway. He leaned in close to her ear. "You mean Holly, right?"

She nodded and they walked swiftly away from Lab One.

Abbie yawned as they walked toward the entrance to the Quantum Lab Array Building. "Let's swing by the QuESO so I can put these away and then go check on things in my temporary apartment."

Sarge exchanged the locker key for their cell phones and bid them goodnight.

"Okay," Joseph put his hand on her back to guide her toward the exit. "Then I'll head into town. My apartment is just fifteen minutes from VEIL. After I take a shower and get cleaned up, we can see if Holly is home."

Abbie sighed. "Uh. I'm exhausted. I'm sure you are too. Why don't you just take an apartment next to mine and save on all the time driving back and forth. I have extra towels and linens."

Joseph yawned. "You know, that's not a bad idea. It's what they are here for. I have some clothes in my office. Let's drop by there and I'll get those."

"Sarge?" Abbie turned to the guard before leaving the building. "Could you arrange for Dr. Assad to get an apartment?"

"Oh sure." He talked on his shoulder mic and by the time they entered the apartment building, a guard was holding a key for Joseph.

They took the elevator up to her floor. Abbie unlocked the door and stepped inside. "I need a shower too."

Joseph smiled. "You want to meet me at the elevator in, say fifteen minutes?"

"Make it twenty, and yes."

Their eyes met and for a moment they were lost in each other's gaze. Joseph leaned closer to her. She closed her eyes anticipating his kiss.

"Excuse me!" Another security guard bounded down the hall. Abbie jumped back from Joseph. The guard looked exhausted.

"Get a room." The guard growled as he strode past them, continuing down the hall.

"I did, actually." Joseph called out to his retreating form. Abbie laid her forehead against Joseph's shoulder and giggled.

Twenty minutes later, Abbie hurried down the hall. Joseph looked up as she approached. "You look better."

"Better?"

"Not as dusty."

"Oh." She smiled. "Let's go see if Holly's in her apartment."

They rode the elevator down to the first floor and turned to their left to Holly's apartment. Joseph knocked. "I've only been here once. She had me pick up some Entanglement text book she had been quoting all day." He chuckled. "She co-authored with Dr. Cooper from my alma mater."

"She co-authored a text book with a prof from The University of Texas?"

Joseph's brow rose. "Yes. It was the basis for a lot of her ideas she dreamed up here."

Abbie pursed her lips. "Interesting."

Joseph knocked again, but the door opened against the pressure of his knuckle. He looked at Abbie, then peeked around the door. "Holly?"

Abbie looked past him. "Holly? You alright?" She stepped in, still looking around. Joseph looked past the bar separating the kitchen from the living room. "She's not in the kitchen."

Abbie hurried to the short hall and looked in the

bathroom and the bedroom. "She's not over here either."

"Where could she be?"

"I don't know." Abbie looked around. "It looks like her apartment was ransacked."

Joseph chucked. "No. It looked this way last time I was here."

Abbie nodded. Just then a sound caught their attention, they turned toward the door.

"Oh. Axel." Abbie sighed. "Is Holly with you?"

"Yes." Axel stepped back into the hall and drew Holly into her apartment. "What are you two doing here?"

"We came by to see how Holly was… and the door was open." Joseph stepped around Abbie. "Is anything missing, or…"

"I don't think so." Holly swept the room with a confirming look. "No. Nothing looks out of place."

"Really?" Abbie followed Holly's sweep. "Well. Why was your door open?"

Axel turned to Holly. "Did we leave the door unlocked?"

Holly shrugged. "I thought you would get into trouble if you talked to me."

"Frankly, we don't care. We've got questions and only you can answer them." Abbie flopped down on the sofa.

Holly's brow raised. "Alright. Let's talk."

They reviewed what Abbie had found in her

discoveries. Joseph talked about what he suspected with the explosion marks. Axel and Holly shared what they suspected. Abbie couldn't shake the feeling they were not telling her and Joseph everything, but then again, she didn't tell them about her faeries or what the girls had said about the rock wall on their side of the dimensional veil.

However, the four of them talked until it was dark.

Eventually, they yawned more than they spoke, and Joseph suggested they go to their respective apartments.

"Good idea. I'm really tired." Holly walked her guest to the door.

"Me too." Abbie took Joseph's elbow. "Escort me home?"

He nodded with a smile. "I'd be honored."

They walked to the elevator while Axel lingered in Holly's apartment. Perhaps he was getting his goodnight kiss. Abbie smiled at Joseph. "I find that I like Holly when she is with Axel."

"What do you mean?"

"I don't know… she seems different when she's around him. Maybe he's good for her and vise versa."

"I can relate to that." He smiled. They slowly rode the elevator to the third floor. Joseph walked her to her door. Once she unlocked her door, she turned to Joseph.

"Good night, Dr. Assad."

"Good night. Sleep tight." Joseph opened her door and

watched her enter. "I'll come get you in the morning."

"Thank you."

He kissed her sweetly then closed her door.

Abbie hugged herself and drew in a deep breath, she let it out as she spun around and walked straight to the bedroom. The two faeries flew out of the doll house and the others rose into the air. "We missed you."

Abbie smiled. "I missed you too. Are you hungry?"

Chapter Fifteen

"I want my faeries back!" Layla snarled as she paced back and forth in front of the shimmering quartz wall. A small dragon-lizard scurried out of her path just before her foot slammed down on its spiny dorsal. It turned and hissed a spark of fire toward her satin shoe, then ran for cover.

A thread binding a delicate onyx bead to her slipper in a floral design sizzled. The bead fell to the ground and rolled away from her foot. A micro-sized gerbil with bony plates protruding from its back like a tiny stegosaurus and horns like a ram sat up on its haunches, then bounced out from under the dank leaves to grab the bead. He shoved it into a tiny leather pouch at its side, and hustled back under its cover.

"They are mine to command! How dare they leave my kingdom? They belong to Velona!" She shook her fist at the scintillating crystalized outcrop. The sheet had not been present in her queendom just two days ago.

A silhouette eased into view. Layla silenced and crept closer. Had that pink-headed rock-gatherer come back to taunt her with more discussions about her faeries? If she could just reach through this crack, she could pull them back into Velona! She lifted her hand, intending to stick a long, sharp nail into the fissure. A burning sensation zapped her fingertip and she jerked back. Her body wafted into a vapor of wet mud, then blinked into a wall of fire. She gritted her teeth, bringing her form back to the preferred body of a queen.

"Ow!" She staggered back, shaking the pain from her hand. Rubbing her arm to dispel the ache that lingered in her lean muscles. She glared at the ominous sliver. There was a power in the fracture that prevented her from touching it. The seal of her banishment had not been broken even after all these years.

She tilted her head. The dark silhouette crept closer. It was not the pink-haired woman. It was a man silhouetted against the crystalized wall. Could it be the same man she had seen, felt, was drawn to when she first stood here gazing at this phenomenal incident in her queendom?

He *had* returned.

She smiled. He could be useful.

She shook back her hair, letting it cascade over her shoulders as beauty replaced her true image. Falling from her like dark, dead scales tumbling from a snake. Her transformation cascaded with her beautiful hair, one scale at a time, until she stood as a radiant woman in a creamy-white silken Grecian gown.

She blinked orange slitted eyes, which morphed into lovely rounded violet irises. Her sharp blood-sucking teeth, gnashed with a snap of her jaw, into glistening white pearls of a well-bred goddess. She closed her eyes once again and mustered forth tears.

"I wonder?" She spoke meekly, positioning her eye near the slight opening. She could just see the man's ruggedly handsome, sun-bronzed face. "Do you know what has happened here? I-I'm so frightened. Please don't hurt me, demon."

The man leaned closer to the crack. "No. I'm no demon, ma'am. I'm not sure what has happened, but it is a strange phenomenon here, too."

She sniffed back tears. "Did you lose your loved one also?"

"Well, yes. We lost a good man." The black island in the center of his startlingly blue eye widened as he peered through the hole. It looked like a whirlpool in a clear lake which reflected a cloudless sky. "Who have you lost, ma'am."

Layla jerked her head back, tossing it from side to side. Where was this *man*? What was this 'here too' that he spoke of. Could this 'good man' come through to her Velona? She would not have this! Her body flashed into a streak of molten lava. She gritted her teeth, bringing herself back into the form she desired. Shaking back the beautiful long hair, she approached the intrusive wall. "I fear we have lost many from my… our world. There are many missing." She swallowed with difficulty. "I heard a loud noise. Like a mountain had fallen into the sea. I rushed down here to see if my… subjects were harmed. But all I found was this strange wall of glimmering stone" —she leaned back letting her eyes rove over the quartz partition— "It was not here before."

She blinked, feeling her eyes contort and return to the beautiful violet, human eyes. "You say one of your kind has come through… to here?"

"We're not sure, ma'am." He looked past her. Was he searching for his missing comrade?

"You *loved* this 'good man' you lost?" She suppressed the gag reflex that came with the loathsome word.

He jerked back. "No! He's an employee. A good man. We don't know what happened to him, but he's no longer here."

"Where is… here." Her brow peaked. Could this be what she hoped?

"Well, I guess you'd say this is Earth. Where are you?"

She stared at him. Her tears pooled and spilled over her lashes. "Here is where I have been for a… very long time. I too am lost from Earth." She tenderly wiped a tear. "I call this Velona."

He leaned against the solid rock wall. Concern, confusion, even fear cascaded from his persona. She tilted her head, deciphering the meaning of these strangely entangled emotions. Deceit! But who was he deceiving?

"Ma'am there have been… creatures come through this… well, we aren't sure how they are getting into our world. We were conducting a… full-scale test, a, uh, experiment. The results were… different than expected. I, uh, some unusual creatures have wandered into our world, that's for certain."

"Oh." She sobbed, disguising her gritted teeth. How dare her subjects leave Velona! "I was afraid of that! This is dreadful! My poor dear ones!" She sobbed the louder.

A dark silhouette of his hand pressed against the wall. She put her hand over his on her side of the rock. His eyes smiled.

"Have you seen… my faeries? They are so delicate, the dear creatures. I feel terrible. They are too curious for their own good—" She gulped as if holding back a sob. "I sent them on a mission to gather berries. Just a task to allow them to feel useful. Oh, what have I done? I sent them to their doom!" She buried her face in her hands. "I can't imagine what happened to them. Please!" She looked up, projecting desperation in her eyes. "Can you help me find them?"

"Faeries? Here? I don't know. What we did see was

huge… and alone." The man's voice sounded too eager. She loathed him already.

"I've convinced everyone it was just a bear— Do you know what a bear is?"

She paused. "I recall the animal of which you speak. Lions and bears, *snakes* in trees, forbidden fruit." She snarled then regained her composure. "I knew the animals of your kingdom."

"Who are you?" The man begged.

She tossed her head back, amused by his curiosity. Leaning in closer, her eyes focused on the crack. She considered how to answer his multidimensional question. Was the fissure getting wider? Could there be hope that she would eventually step through, to regain her rightful place among the humans from whom she had been proscribed?

"Me? I am but a humble Queen in this land. Who might you be? You look to me to be of noble blood. Are you a king?"

The man breathed in her flattery like the foolish human she took him to be. "No. My name is Stettler, Adam Stettler."

She stiffened. "Adam, you say." Stepping back she gathered herself to keep from revealing her innermost desires. Her heart ached for the one she lost so many years ago. "I once knew a man named Adam, are you his descendent?"

The man chuckled. "No, my father is… well that's not his name. May I ask you a question?"

"I could not refuse one as handsome as you. Ask your question."

"Like I said, an unusual… being has come from where you are. Yet, I see you standing there. You look lovely, normal. Are you a human? Can you just walk through to my side of this wall?"

Layla seethed, sucking saliva through her teeth. This was the very issue she had sent that mongrel Anak to discover. Could this naïve mortal man give her the answers her feeble servant could not?

She whimpered a lamenting cry. "I don't know. It is why I stand here, looking for my lost cherubs. I cannot get to them. I *must* know that they are safe? I pray no one on your side of this… this wall has harmed them?"

"Ma'am I haven't seen any faeries. But we lost sight of a large figure—"

"Oh! My darling faeries! I heard that… woman speak of them!"

"I don't know. What woman?"

"She has hair the color of a pomegranate. She stood at this very wall, making a horrible scraping noise. My teeth were set on edge with her incessant scraping."

"I think I know this woman. She's is a geologist and I assigned her to investigate this phenomenon, to discover what has happened here." He turned his eye to peer through the crack. "You say she spoke of your faeries? Like real faeries? Tinker Bell-like faeries?"

"I know not this *Tinker Bell* creature, but yes my faeries are delicate little creatures, about this big." She shook her hand and then held up a delicate finger and thumb demonstrating about three inches.

That rock gatherer! Layla gnashed her teeth and curled her lips. Just as quickly she relaxed and resumed her beautiful composure. "Yes, the poor dears. They are so frightfully dependent, they cling to anyone who seems to be kind to them. They are not intelligent enough to know when they are a nuisance. I'm so sorry for their behavior. Please! Apologize for me when you find them… to her." She peered through the fissure. "If you could bring them to me, I would reward you handsomely. Up to half my kingdom shall be yours, if only you could return my precious faeries to me."

Adam's eyes widened. He seemed to ponder a thought. "You mean, I could— no, that would be crazy!"

"What? Ask and it shall be granted, once you bring my precious faeries back to me."

"Your eyes are beautiful, my Queen." He leaned into the fissure. She stepped back to let him observe her beauty. His eyes darted around, taking in her queendom. "I have this… stirring in my heart that cannot be explained. I want to bring you whatever your heart desires. If it is faeries you wish, I will bring them to you. I ask only that you allow me to cross over into your world, perhaps. If I am unable to resolve some issues here, that might be the perfect solution for me. Yes. I could… just disappear." He stepped away and then returned. "Would you be agreeable to letting me come live in your world?"

She gawked at him. The nerve! "Yes." She hissed. A vision of him stepping through a fissure, handing her a cage with the faeries trembling inside. She would take the cage with her left hand and stab him in the heart with her right. He would die astonished at her feet as she laughed, holding up the caged faeries.

He picked a fingernail at the sliver that remained open between their worlds. "I don't seem to be able to enter your world. But I will find a way. I promise you, I will find a way, and I will bring you those faeries."

She grinned. "Thank you my kind, mysterious prince."

His silhouette faded.

"What a fool! He fell for every lie!" She spat the words like bitter poison from her mouth. "Like I'd share one boulder of my queendom with the unfaithful species of man." She turned with a flourish and plodded her way back to her castle.

"Anak!" She summoned her servant to her side through the linking tendrils of his mind. He had better have information.

Chapter Sixteen

Abbie leaned on the counter, slowly blinking the sleep from her eyes. She drew her robe tighter across her pajamas. The coffee pot groaned and sighed a final puff of steam. She inhaled and poured herself that first cup of heaven. The toaster popped. She turned and buttered both slices. One she covered with honey, the other she spread a thin coat of blackberry jam. Carrying the cup and toast to a stool, she sat down, and sipped her coffee while the faeries devoured the honey-saturated slice of bread.

She pulled a Petri dish from her purse and filled it with sweet cream. The faeries took turns bending over the liquid like kittens. Abbie smiled. They were so cute.

A knock came to her door. "Who could that be?" She carried her coffee to the door and pulled it open. "Yes, may I help— Oh!"

"Room service, Miss." Joseph purred his lovely hispanic accent and held up two recyclable grocery sacks.

"Joseph! What did you bring?" Abbie leaned to kiss his cheek.

Joseph paused with his bags still held aloft. "Hmm. Keep that up and you'll never get breakfast."

"Well, then, do come in. I promise to behave." Abbie intentionally let her hips swing as she walked ahead of him. She was shameless around him. She flipped a hand toward the lounging faeries on the counter, sleepily blinking and rubbing their tummies. "I can't guarantee their behavior though."

Joseph chuckled uncomfortably, putting his bags on the counter next to the stove. "Pancakes, bacon, eggs, and…" He looked at the faeries, who eagerly listened, rubbing their hands together. Joseph hesitated, but then followed through. "Cinnamon churros."

The faeries jumped up, squealing with delight.

"Wait a minute." Abbie rounded her shoulders. "You just ate an entire slice of bread with honey and butter. Now you're going to eat churros?"

"Yes!" They sprang into the air, landing next to Joseph and his white sack of Mexican pastries. He leaned back from them, with concern in his face.

Abbie tsked her tongue. "Well it's a good thing you have the metabolism of a hummingbird." She laughed and turned to Joseph. "Thanks, but I just had my toast and coffee."

Joseph's smile dropped. "That's all you eat for breakfast?"

"Usually."

He shook his head. "How do you keep from fainting without a good breakfast?"

"I keep very well, thank you… without expanding to where I can't wear any of my clothes." She giggled.

"Alright." Joseph drew her into his arms, glancing at the faeries, then returning his gaze to her eyes. "Do you mind if I make myself a plate of bacon and eggs? Maybe one churro?" He glanced at the voracious faeries. "If they leave me one. I promise to wash the dishes."

Aura stood, sheepishly, and struggled to lift a churro toward Joseph. He took it with a circumspect nod of thanks.

Abbie smiled, leaning back from his embrace, his arms still encircling her waist. She looked him squarely in the face. "Be my guest."

He leaned closer to her, touching his nose to hers like an Eskimo kiss, all the while gazing deeply into her eyes. His lips brushed hers. She wrapped her arms around him and ran her fingers into his hair, pulling him closer, deeper as passion exploded in her heart. He returned her passion, running his hand up and down her back, covering her mouth with his. Her mind reeled, her passion soared. She wanted so much more!

"Awwww." The faeries cooed.

Abbie turned her head toward them. They stood with their hands serpentined under their chin, enthralled by watching their passionate exchange. Abbie blinked, stepped out of Joseph's embrace, and cleared her throat.

"Coffee?" She tucked a strand of pink hair behind her ear.

"Was that… real? Or was it—" He glared at the enamored faeries. "Yes, please." He turned to the cabinet and reached for the frying pan, visibly shaken by their sudden bout of passion.

Abbie returned to her stool and watched him deftly prepare the meal.

"So… I have some news you are not going to like." Joseph glanced over his shoulder.

Abbie sat up straighter. "What?"

"Well, it seems Axel and Holly were arrested last night."

"What? How?" She slammed her coffee cup down. "You should have led with that!"

"Well. It seems they found out where the power coupling had been, um, stored, and they went exploring. Rick Sharp and some of the guards found them… what's the saying?" He held out his hands. "Red handed?"

Abbie nodded. "Yeah that's right if you mean they caught them with the coupling."

"Yes. That's what I mean."

"We were just with them last night! Are they alright?" Abbie swallowed.

Joseph grimaced. "I think so. After we left, I guess they decided to go investigate the damage."

"Axel's the very person who should be assigned to examine that thing! None of this makes sense."

"I know." Joseph turned the bacon over.

Abbie inhaled. "Mmmm that smells good."

"See…" he turned with a beautiful grin across his face. "You are hungry."

She tilted her head coyly. "Am I terrible to want one piece of bacon when our friends are locked up? Are they in the town jail?"

"No. Actually, they locked them up in this historical jail commissioned by VEIL. I don't think anybody conceived that we'd ever need a brig for any reason, and so I hear it's pretty antiquated. I can't imagine it actually holding a guy like Axel." Joseph glanced up at her. "I have a feeling whatever charges they are being held for will not stick. And I already put an extra strip in the pan, hoping you would eat it."

She held up her coffee as a salute to his thoughtfulness and took another sip of her morning brew. "Oh really. Why do I think you and Axel have something up your sleeve?"

"No. Not up my sleeve. But we do have something that is going to work in their favor."

Abbie squinted at him. "And, I guess you can't tell me?"

"No. Not right now, but soon."

She nodded with uncertainty. "Okay…"

"So, what's your game plan this morning?" Joseph plated the food and brought it to sit beside her. The faeries remained by the stove, surrounded by churros crumbs.

"I want to get back into Lab One. If Axel is out of commission, I wonder if Sharp will be there? Maybe I should take the faeries and get their feedback on the—"

"No!" The faeries flittered into flight and zoomed from the kitchen to their doll house. "We not go near that wall." "Mother Righteous is there." "She will see us." "She will make us go back." "And punish us." "She knows we were the ones." "We were making a rebellion against her." "Velona on their own." "We stay here." "Safe here." "Love is here."

Abbie turned away from their complaining. "There's something about that fissure that draws my attention."

Joseph tore his eyes off the fury of the faeries. "What are you thinking?"

Abbie put her coffee cup down. "I'm thinking it's getting bigger. Like the quartz is decaying or crumbling and making it bigger." She stared at her cup. "I've measured it three times, and I know it's getting wider."

"What do you think that means? Other than the obvious."

"Well, as terrified as the girls are of Mother Righteous,

and being forced to go back through… and that eye belonged to somebody who scared the bageezies out of me the other day… I think sometime soon there will be an opening big enough to climb or even walk through."

Joseph nodded. "And you are afraid this Mother Righteous will walk through and snatch the faeries?"

"Well." Abbie lifted her cup and drank the cooled coffee. "Yes, but more than that, I'm thinking we can send a team through—"

Joseph sat up straighter.

"To find Zeke." They said at the same time.

Abbie nodded with a smile. "Right!"

"Of course. Excellent!" Joseph finished the last of his meal and put the plate in the sink. He washed all the dishes while Abbie went to her bedroom and finished getting dressed for work.

"Ready?"

"Ready." Abbie pulled her purse over her shoulder and turned to the still complaining faeries in the doll house. "So, you girls stay here. I'll come get you when we move to my office."

"Don't go to that wall!" Aura begged.

"Aura, I have my job to do. I'll be safe. Joseph is with me."

Aura pouted with a shrug. "Layla has… bad powers. She can hurt you when she is angry."

Abbie carried her canvas tool bag over her shoulder and followed Joseph into Lab One. Aura's warning clinging to her nerves. She wanted to get more readings from the event site. Everyday the fog and the illuminating effect from the entanglement seemed to remain the same, but that fissure— got bigger. Why? Was it under pressure, decaying, or… was someone or something causing it to widen? Who could be doing that? Stettler had given limited access to the lab. She, Joseph, Axel, and Sharp were the only people allowed to work in there, as far as she knew.

But did she know everything Stettler had ordered? Of course not! She jerked to a halt with a gasp.

"What?" Joseph turned with her sudden stop.

Abbie looked around. No one was near enough to hear her speak to Joseph. "What if…" She stepped closer to him, leaning as if to kiss his cheek and spoke softly into his ear. "What if someone is chiseling at the fissure and that's what's causing it to widen? Could it be that Stettler ordered someone to work on it at night, when we leave the lab? Or maybe it's happening on the other side? Maybe other… *creatures* are trying to break the quartz wall?"

Joseph's brow pressed down in thought. "Is that really what you think?"

"I'm not sure. I'm just trying to analyze my findings in my head. Nothing about that fog or that scintillating wall is any different since the… accident. But that crack measures wider every time we measure it. Something is happening to it. I just don't know what. The simplest answer is that someone is going in there and chipping at it but why? And who?" Abbie licked her lips and swallowed. The memory of that snake-like eye suddenly appearing, the fear that overwhelmed her, like a backflash fireball. Could that creature be trying to get through by tearing down the wall?

"If it's something from the other side, why doesn't it just come through like the faeries, or that big creature? Obviously they came through… somehow, without crawling through the crack." She glared at Joseph with deep concentration.

"And whatever happened to that big creature?" Joseph looked deep in thought too.

"Haven't heard anything?"

He shook his head. "Me neither. I've spent all my time with you. I haven't heard anything. It's not like people are posting pictures on Facebook or anything." He chuckled, but the humor didn't reach his eyes.

"Or Instagram." She chuckled. "But I was hoping you'd heard something. Have any more creatures come through?"

He shrugged. "You're right, though. The fissure was

barely a cleavage in the quartz when the faeries appeared. Somehow they just penetrated through and came out of the fog, or… like you've said, maybe it *is* the fog. Maybe *it* is the portal. And you're right about that snake-eyed creature, it doesn't seem to be able to simply pass through like these other creatures. *Es muy raro*."

Abbie giggled. "Rare, indeed."

She continued walking to Lab One. The room was silent and empty. An eery sensation raised goosebumps on her arms. "Man, it's weird without Axel and Rick in here working."

"I wonder how long they'll keep Axel and Holly in jail?" Joseph looked around as if he might see them working behind a large piece of equipment.

Abbie shrugged. "Like I said, it doesn't even make sense they'd be arrested for trying to inspect the power coupling?"

"No. It does not."

"Maybe we should talk to Sheriff Spotted Wolf. As character witnesses, maybe we can convince her that Axel and Holly are being judged too harshly. Maybe it's time somebody knew about how strange Stettler is acting."

"That's what I was thinking too."

"Okay, let's get these measurements and… wait! I can't leave the facility."

"Why not?" Joseph's brow pressed into a deep furrow.

"The faeries can't leave the facility. You can go wherever you want."

"But if Stettler finds out the faeries exist... I just can't imagine— well, yes I can. They will become the object of study and won't have any kind of life outside of a laboratory."

"How is that different from what you are providing for them?"

Abbie's eyes widened and her jaw dropped. "I-I'm protecting them, not keeping them as a science experiment!"

"I know, but what freedom do they have?"

Abbie stared at the floor. "You make a good point. But I don't know what else to do for now."

"How about this? I will go to town and talk to Sheriff Spotted Wolf."

She nodded. "Yeah, that's a good plan. I'll get the girls. For some reason I feel I want them near me and not left alone in the apartment. I can use the roller cart to transport the doll house to my office while I write up my findings. I honestly think it's safer."

He nodded. "Okay."

Abbie walked up to the still sparkling wall, immersed by the ever-present fog. Something crunched under her feet. She squatted to get a better look, setting her canvas bag on the floor. Fallen rocks of varying sizes, from slivers to the size of a quarter, scattered the floor. Was this evidence someone had been chiseling at the fissure or was it something else? She touched Joseph's pant leg and tipped her head toward the debris.

He knelt down. "Could the fog be degrading the quartz, and causing it to crumble?"

"Water can make its way through just about any medium and cause damage. Think of Carlsbad Caverns. That was a completely enclosed environment, and yet water seeped in and formed all those amazing stalactites and stalagmites. But that takes years, centuries. This is happening in a matter of days."

"True." Joseph stood, looking closely at the darker purple rock that surrounded the fissure.

Abbie nodded. Her mind reeling over ideas of what could be causing this crack to grow larger each day. "I've recorded a gradual enlarging of this fissure, but—" She looked directly into Joseph eyes. "This looks different."

Joseph nodded. "Let's get our readings and get on with our other errands."

Abbie lifted her metal ruler while Joseph lifted the clipboard. Together they measured the width of the increasing fissure from left to right. At about the half-way point, Joseph paused. "Do you hear something?"

Abbie tilted her head, listening. "A rhythmic… muffled clomping sound. It seems like it's getting closer."

"Sí. If I didn't know better, I would say it was a

hoofed animal… a horse running toward—"

A large, dark shadow fell across the quartz wall. Joseph grabbed Abbie's shoulders and pulled her back as a smoky-gray horse sprang through the wall as if the rock wall were nothing more than a holographic image. The fog sparkled brighter and swirled around the horse's hooves and tail as it passed by them.

Abbie stared at the mangy coat and dry, splintered hooves of the beast that nearly trampled her. Froth peeled off its back, like soap. What was it running from?

Its fear-filled eye met her gaze, turned to its right, and charged out the corridor toward the forested mountain. Abbie stood in shocked silence, with Joseph holding her. She could feel his heart beat wildly against her back.

"Holy Cow!" Abbie pressed against Joseph's muscular chest.

"Nope, I'd say that was a horse," Joseph answered flatly.

Abbie chortled. "Yeah, but where did it go?"

"I have no idea."

"Well, that answers one question." She turned around to face him. Their eyes locked and for a moment Abbie lost her thought in the caramel depths of his dark eyes. She cleared her throat. "They're not coming through the fissure."

Joseph touched a tendril of her bangs, pushing it away from her brow. "That's good to know." He lowered his face to hers, closing his eyes, his lips pressed onto hers. She pulled back. "We-we need to-to get this done."

He swallowed. "You're right. I'm sorry."

"No. No apologies necessary. I felt it too." She smiled. "And this time we know for sure it wasn't the faeries."

"Sí." He touched the solid quartz wall. "And yet, we still don't know if it's the entangled quartz or the fog that's letting the aliens through."

Abbie turned back to the scintillating wall. "Aliens?" She chuckled. "Okay, true." She, too, tested the solidity of the quartz. "But did you notice how bright the sparkling lights got when that animal came through. Now, it's not so luminescent."

"You're right." Joseph continued to inspect the quartz. He knocked on the rock with his knuckles. "It's solid as a rock." He smiled. "You know, so how did that beast get through it?"

"This portion of the wall is a portal." She gestured a huge circle. "That's all I know. And it seems to be a one-way portal. Does that even make sense?"

"Dimensional pathways are theories. This is the first that I know of for anyone to study." His eyes roved over the glittery wall. "Wait. Let me try something." He bent to pick up a sliver of broken quartz. Standing, he pushed it through the fissure. It fell to the other side. "I am sooo writing a paper about this!"

Abbie smiled. His eagerness warmed her heart. "Me, too!"

The lab phone rang. Abbie jumped away from Joseph. "Should we answer that?"

"I guess so. We're the only ones in here."

It rang again.

Abbie hurried across the lab to the desk. "Lab One, Dr. Abbie Crossan."

"Dr. Crossan?" Director Stettler's secretary, Melissa, sounded anxious. "Is Dr. Assad with you?"

"Yes." Abbie turned to look at Joseph. "We were told to partn—"

"Yeah, sure. Listen, Director Stettler needs you two in his office, ASAP."

"Okay? What's this about?"

"I'm not sure. Just following orders. You know how he gets."

"Sure, Melissa. Are you alright?"

"Yeah. It's just been a tough several days."

"Okay. We'll clean up and head that way."

"Please don't take too long. He's… well you know…" She apparently cupped her hand over her mouth and the phone to speak more directly into the receiver. "He's hyper-skitzoid today."

Abbie laughed. "Okay. We'll hurry." She hung up. "Stettler wants us in his office. You don't suppose it has to do with Axel and Holly, do you?"

"No idea." Joseph put the clipboard in her canvas tool bag and lifted it to his shoulder. "Maybe he found out we were kissing in here and now we'll be grounded from seeing each other."

Abbie's eyes darted around the lab. Were there security cameras? "That's not funny. I wouldn't put anything past our Director. He's been so weird ever since the accident."

"Well, one thing I do know"

"What?"

"The sooner we get to his office, the sooner we'll know what he wants."

Abbie sighed. "Yeah. Should we tell him about the horse?"

"Oh, hell no!" Joseph touched her back to guide her out of the lab. "Don't tell him anything about faeries or horses, or... No that's all. Right? We should *play it cool*— is that the term? And see what happens."

She jerked her head to look at him. "Should we go check on the girls first?"

"No, she said ASAP, I think we should just go straight there."

"Okay." Anxiety roiled in her gut. This didn't feel right. "It's just... I have a weird feeling..."

Joseph pursed his lips. "Me, too."

Chapter Seventeen

"Oh, Abbie!" Melissa leapt from her chair to greet Abbie and Joseph as they walk into Stettler's outer office. "I'm so sorry. I told you to get right over here and now he's gone… somewhere. I have no idea where. He just said to tell you to wait in his office and he'll be right back." She grimaced. "I'm so sorry."

"It's alright, Melissa. You don't have any control over your boss. We were finished with what we were doing in Lab One anyway." Abbie patted her shoulder.

Melissa nodded. "That's good." She seemed to be breathing too fast. "Okay, well, go on in. Can I get you coffee… or anything while you wait?"

"No." Abbie looked at Joseph. He didn't indicate he wanted anything. "We're fine."

They walked into Stettler's office and sat down. Joseph gestured to his ear and pointed at his desk.

Abbie shrugged and put her finger over her lips.

Joseph nodded. There was no telling whether the director's office was bugged. Just to be safe they didn't speak. Joseph sat with both feet flat on the floor, his arms casually on the arm rests. He looked around, but remained silent.

Abbie shifted in her chair, crossed her legs, and waited. Her eyes swept his office. A large, split-in-half geode sat on his credenza. Its pink spiky crystals matched the color of the wall she had been studying so intensely the past few days. Minus the entangled light show, of course. She sighed. A clock on the wall ticked.

Stettler's phone rang. Melissa could be heard answering it from her office. "Director Adam Stettler's office, this is Melissa."

She told the caller he was out of the office and she'd be happy to take a message. She was a good secretary, efficient. Abbie liked her as a friend, although she'd spent very little time with her, other than happenstance encounters at The Oasis. Perhaps she should do better and invite her over when this was settled and she could go back home.

Home. Would she ever be able to go home as long as the faeries were attached to her? She sighed.

Joseph caught her eye. He smiled, sympathetically, but said nothing.

Abbie leaned in her chair to look in Melissa's office. She could just see the door. Where was Stettler? People walked down the hall. No one seemed alarmed or excited. What did Stettler want? Why did it no longer seem so urgent? What was so important to leave them waiting here like this?

Thirty minutes passed. Abbie stood. Joseph watched her with knitted brow. "This is ridiculous. If he still wants to talk to me, he can come to my office. Let's go."

Joseph stood. "Alright."

"Melissa." Abbie crossed the outer office. "Tell Stettler I'll be in my office getting work done that *he ordered* me to do." Abbie continued out into the hall. Melissa's voice trailed behind her. "But—"

Joseph followed. Once they stepped into the sunlight, Abbie shook her head. "I cannot believe the nerve of that man!"

"That seemed odd to me. Did it to you?"

"Odd?" Abbie gawked at him as they walked toward the QuESO building. "It was rude." They entered the indigenous garden and continued along the crushed granite walkway. "It was almost like—

"He lured us away from the lab?" Joseph completed her thought.

"Or—" She touched his arm. "Joseph! You don't think he... found out about the faeries?"

"How would he?" Joseph took a step off the granite path, away from the Environment building, to cross the garden.

"I don't know. Maybe someone saw... and told him?" Abbie looked toward her apartment.

"Don't panic!" Joseph broke into a run. Abbie ran at his heals. They dashed in the side door and bolted up the three flights of stairs.

Her apartment door was open.

"No, no, no, no!" Abbie panted. She shoved against the door and stumbled into her apartment. The faeries flitted furiously in the space around the doll house.

Abbie sighed in relief.

Diamond spotted Abbie and squeaked, "He took Aura!"

All the faeries dashed toward Abbie. "We fought him!" "He tried to take us!" "Aura was brave!" "But he caught her!" "We smashed his eye!"

"What?" Abbie coughed. "Who?" She feared she knew exactly who.

"The one called Stettler!" They all said as one.

Abbie collapsed to her knees. "He tricked us!" The faeries followed her down swing and swooped into her hair. They trembled with anger and fear.

"It's alright." She cooed. "He's probably taken her to security. We'll go talk to him."

"NO!" The faerics screamed as loud as their little voices could carry. "He said he was taking her to Mother Righteous!"

Joseph's eyes went wide. "What? Why would he do that?"

"Mother Righteous told him to bring us!" "We have to save Aura." "Mother Righteous will hurt Aura." "She is very angry." "We left Velona." "We have to go back…" "And save Aura."

Diamond flew in front of Abbie's face. She looked stiff, determined. "We have to go back. We were gathering a rebellion. But now, we have to finish our mutiny against that false Queen."

The faeries began speaking at once. "She is evil!" "We must rescue Aura." "Layla will hurt her."

Abbie looked at Joseph but spoke to the faeries. "I thought you were too afraid of this Queen Layla to go back to Velona?"

Several more faeries joined Diamond in front of Abbie. "She is no Queen!" "She is no mother!" "We must help Aura!" "And stop Layla!"

"Well. Alright." Abbie stood. "Then we'll take you to the wall. If that fissure isn't big enough for you to get through, we'll make it bigger." Abbie lifted her canvas tool bag and marched to her door. "You coming?"

Joseph nodded. "We have to be cautious. Stettler may be there now?"

"You're right. Maybe we should go in from the broken wall on the side of the mountain."

"Good thinking." Joseph put his hand on her shoulder and turned her to face him. "Abbie, you are an amazing woman, and… I love you."

Her eyes widened. "I-I love you, too. But let's get these faeries through the wall and talk about that afterward."

His eyes darted to the remaining faeries buried in Abbie's hair. "You're right, as usual. But—" He stopped her from walking away. "It's not the faeries. I'm serious. You are an amazing woman. I love you. And whatever happens with these… faeries, I don't want our 'partnering up' to end."

"Oh gosh! Joseph, I can't deal with this right now. We've got to take care of this crisis. You understand? I'm not saying no. I'm just—"

"No. I get it. Let's go." Joseph placed his hand on her back and together they hurried to the side of the Quantum Entanglement Physics Labs building. They scurried up the ascending grade toward where the Lab One explosion opened into the forested area.

Abbie paused. "Before we do this, can I just take a moment to say something?"

The faeries flew out of her hair and between her and Joseph. "We know. This is where we first met."

"Yes." Tears sprang to Abbie's eyes. "I'm going to miss you. All of you. But… you have a mission. I understand that. And I want Aura safe, too. Don't tell her I said this, but I think she was my favorite."

"She is our leader." "She is strong." "She is our

favorite, too." The faeries wiped their tiny eyes. "We will miss you, Abbie." "We learned love from you." "We love love."

"Yes." Abbie chuckled. "I know." She smiled at Joseph. He returned her amusement.

"Be careful! If Stettler is still down there… I do not want you to get caught!"

"We will be careful."

They swarmed her face, each kissing her cheek. It felt like tiny pin pricks, but she loved it. "Okay. Quiet as a mouse, let's go."

Abbie gingerly put her foot forward and silently crept into the side of the Lab One. Stettler was not there, but as she neared the entangled wall she saw something alarming.

"Look!" she whispered.

Joseph followed her line of sight. The fractured fissure was the size of a corsage box. Someone had been here, and broken it open. "Do you suppose Stettler put Aura in a small box and…" Abbie could barely make herself say the words. "Gave her to Layla?"

"It looks that way." Joseph's sad eyes met Abbie's. "I'm so sorry."

The faeries flew to the hole in the scintillating wall. They perched on the jagged quartz.

"Mother Ri— Layla has been here." Diamond looked terrified. "Aura is imprisoned."

"How do you know that?" Abbie looked past them into the land they called Velona. Then she felt their glare. She focused her sight on them. They all stared at her like she'd forgotten who they were. "You can hear her?"

Diamond touched a teeny finger to her head. "Yes. In here. We have to go."

"Yes." Abbie swallowed, fighting the emotions that balled at her throat, holding her voice captive. "Be careful. Good luck. Remember me," she croaked.

"We will never forget you, Abbie." Diamond turned. She lifted her arms over her head and dove into Velona like an Olympic diver. The others followed her. Abbie watched them fly away until she couldn't see them anymore. To her right, far away in Velona, high on a mountain, as if it were above a cloud, she saw a dark castle structure. Was that where Layla had taken Aura?

Abbie sighed. "Well I hope they are successful!"

"Me too." Joseph took her by the shoulder and turned her to face him. "And, now you are free."

Her eyes widened. "Yeah, I guess I am."

"So." Joseph touched his forehead to hers. "How about you show me your apartment in town?"

She smiled. "I'd love that. And you know what else?"

He put his nose to her nose, gently kissed her lips. "What else?"

"I'd LOVE to take a shower by myself."

He chuckled and covered her mouth with his. Their passion exploded and she buried her hands in his hair behind his head, pulling him deeper into the fervent kiss. Her heart pounded against her ear drums. She loved the way he kissed her and the way her body responded. Without the faeries pressing emotions into them, she knew he was the one she'd always dreamed of. He was her Happy Ever After. The faeries would be missed, but she was grateful she had become entangled with faeries.

THE END

Personal Note from the Author

Who would dye their hair pink and collect Tinker Bell memorabilia? This character was patterned after our daughter-in-law whom we love dearly, pink hair and Tinker Bell-lovin' and all! She makes our son happy and that's all that matters to us! She's not a geologist, but an IT guru. I had to add my own creative flare to the character. :)

When Karole googles what Faeries eat, that information was found at https://www.reference.com/art-literature/fairies-eat-a6f7499e760040de. I kid you not!

Thank you from the bottom of my heart for buying my book. This series, Beyond the VEIL, is so much fun to write in and we, all of who are writing in the series, hope that you are enjoying reading it as much as we enjoyed planning and writing it for you.

The next book in this series is "Entangled by a Faun" by Travis Perry.

Enjoy! God bless you and yours!

Lynn Donovan

Newsletter and Free Book

Hey! Thank you for purchasing and reading my book, Entangled with Faeries. I'd like to give you a parting gift to show my appreciation. To sign up for my newsletter go to www.lynndonovanauthor.com. I will send you an e-copy of a collection of short stories I wrote purely for your entertainment. I will happily send you this e-copy for **FREE**, if you ask. I will also add you to my **NEWSLETTER** list and you will receive up-to-date information on new releases before anyone else.

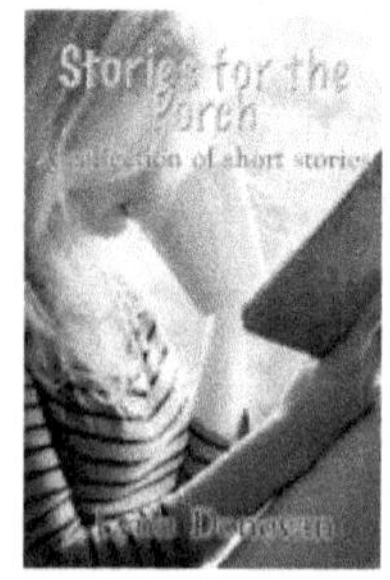

This book will not be sold anywhere, at any time. I am keeping it exclusively for you, my readers.

Thank you again, and God Bless.

~Lynn Donovan